Becoming a Royal Princess

Theastarr Valerie

Empress Royále
Publishing

Editors: Theastarr Valerie, Akilah Valerie
Empress Royále Publishing
Email: empressroyalepublishing@gmail.com

Cover Design: Empress Royále Publishing

Cover Photo: "Gold Crown" from *annielloveslyou* (Pixabay.com)
"Imperial Castle" from *Cold Smiling* (Pixabay.com)

Princess Silhouette: Aleah Valerie, Akilah Valerie

Scriptures verses are taken from the KING JAMES VERSION (KJV): KING JAMES VERSION, Public Domain

Empress Royále Publishing

"Everything tells a story; let us help you tell your story to the world."
Email: empressroyalepublishing@gmail.com

Dedication

To the sons and daughters of the Most High God.

As a child of the King of Kings, you are Royalty.

Never forget who and whose you are.

A heavenly title far outweighs an earthly one.

~Theastarr Valerie

Thank You Heavenly Father for choosing me. I belong to an everlasting Kingdom.

Esther 4:14 (KJV)

"...And who knoweth whether thou art come to the kingdom for such a time as this?"

7 Becoming a Royal Princess

"Keep thy heart with all diligence; for out of it are the issues of life." Proverbs 4:23

Vaia Bisenzo runs behind her *Royal McGovern* suitcase that dropped onto the baggage carousel.

Although she'd been monitoring the carousel, she had a momentary flashback. She wiped the teardrops from her cheeks. This trip was supposed to be for two.

Living in *Lux Point Milano,* Starr Islands, Vaia always dreamed of visiting Europe; **Italy** to be exact. During her school days, she was the only student who smiled when the teacher showed pictures of ancient ruins and artifacts. Now at age 30, her dream finally came true.

Barcelona–El Prat Airport was by far the largest she'd ever traveled to. As she exited the terminal to the shuttle pickup, she exhaled. Eight months had passed since her breakup, but feelings of inadequacy still lingered. Here she was, a single woman, preparing to board the cruise ship alone.

She shrugs off the negative thoughts and begins to smile...

Italy here I come!

Determined not to allow the past to kill her present joy, Vaia submits her passport to the cruise worker.

"Welcome to *Pacitera Luxury Cruise Line,*" the worker greets. "Please follow the signs for boarding."

Vaia heads towards the gangway, knowing that she'd have to wait a while for her luggage.

───⌒───

Getting off the elevator, Vaia walks to room **9377**. Once inside, she plops down on the bed and sobs. The reality of the situation hit her like a ton of bricks: she was **A-L-O-N-E... *ALONE!***

Vaia was the **Queen of Bookworms** to say the least.

While other people found pleasure in merrymaking, cozying up with a good book was her idea of fun.

> *One day she was the heroine trying to save a village from volcanic ash submersion.*

> *The next, she dined with Governor Harnsey in his grand estate.*

There was no stopping her when she opened the pages of a book.

Snapping out of her thoughts, Vaia looks up at the open doorway. A man walks through. She giggles internally as she scans his face. He was definitely handsome.

"Hi, I hope I am not disturbing you," he says, walking towards her.

Even though her focus was not on men, it made Vaia happy to see that good looking ones still existed. Physical attributes alone did not make for a godly husband, but she certainly did not want to wake up next to a *troglodyte* for the rest of her life.

"How are you enjoying the cruise?" the man continues.

Vaia flips her hair and blushes. "It's wonderful."

The man stands over her, making her feel nervous. "What book are you reading?"

"*War of Doors*," she replies, trying to control her racing heart.

"Going to the party tonight?"

"I'm not into partying; at least not the kind on this ship."

"Me neither," the man retorts, sitting next to her. "Do you want to play cards?"

Vaia looks at him, eager to converse with the handsome stranger. "What's your name?"

"Zeno. Yours?"

"Vaia," she giggles.

"Beautiful name. Where are you from?"

"*Lux Point Milano*, Starr Islands."

"Never heard of it," Zeno shrugs.

"You never heard of Starr Islands?"

"I'm not into geography."

Vaia was about to show Zeno a map of Starr Islands, when a woman barges into the room. "There you are, Zeno. I was on the Lido Deck waiting for you."

"I told you that I was coming here to check my emails," Zeno says to the woman.

"**She** doesn't look like **emails** to me," the woman retorts, pointing to Vaia.

Zeno winks at Vaia. "Made a friend."

"Oh, I bet you did," the woman grunts.

He turns to Vaia. "Meet my wife—"

Vaia immediately jumps up from the seat. "W-wife?" she stutters. "I'm sorry miss. I did not know that he's married."

Zeno's wife rolls her eyes. "Hmmmm, I bet you didn't. You fast tailed single chicks are always coming on cruises to snag men. This one's TAKEN. Zeno come on."

"Bye Vaia," Zeno waves. "Sorry about that. She has a short fuse," he chuckles. "Nice meeting you. See you around. Maybe we can actually play that game of cards, without ol' *ball and chain* here."

Vaia stares aghast at the couple leaving the room.

What on earth just happened? How humiliating. Note to self: Do NOT speak to ANY other man on this cruise unless he's taking my dinner order. I need a drama free trip.

Picking up her book, Vaia exits the library, for fear of any other mishaps.

"For the vision is yet for an appointed time, but at the end it shall speak, and not lie: though it tarry, wait for it; because it will surely come, it will not tarry." Habakkuk 2:3

Day Three

When the ship docked in Italy, Vaia signed up for the Livorno-Lucca-Pisa tour. However, May 1st was a holiday in Italy, so shops were closed in Livorno.

After missing her connecting shuttle (through no fault of her own), Vaia joins the remaining passengers left by the bus stop.

Because of the mix-up made by the tour company, a shuttle agent sends the group in a taxi, agreeing to pay any extra fees.

It was not Vaia's original plan, but the *taxi-esque* excursion would turn out to be the best thing that happened to her, she just did not know it yet.

Vaia exits the taxi, noting the time that she had to meet back at the pickup point. The last thing she needed was to be stranded in a foreign country.

With her professional camera in hand, Vaia snaps pictures of the beautiful Tuscan scenery. Pisa was a nice historical stop, but Lucca was where she fell in love with the Italian culture.

Dodging a speeding car, Vaia's mind flashes back to breakfast when she sat at a table next to an elderly couple.

> *"Do you think it will rain?" the man asks Vaia.*
>
> *"No, it will stay this way," Vaia responds, trying to eat her Blossomed Eggs.*
>
> *Outside was gloomy, but no rain fell.*
>
> *"We hope so," the man's wife adds. "Last time we came to Livorno it rained heavily."*
>
> *"I'll hold you to your word that it'll remain like this," the man continued, though Vaia felt like it was a low-key threat.*

I have no idea where I am going.

Unable to read maps, Vaia relied on her ability to recognize landmarks and key signs to direct her.

Walking around *Piazza San Michele*, Vaia ventures into *Passeggiate delle Mura Urbane*. From there she could see the wonderful views of Lucca.

The park was filled with joggers, dog walkers, cyclists, couples holding hands and passengers from the ship.

Things were moving along quite lovely until two things happened:

1. Rain started falling.
2. Vaia felt faintish.

The growling of her stomach signaled apparent hunger. Her throat was drier than a desert. Too bad she left her water bottle and snacks on the ship. Restaurants were a long walk back from the park.

Vaia scoffs in annoyance.

Known for panicking easily, Vaia stops and prays that God would keep her body until she was able to eat. Passing out in a foreign country was not an option.

Thankfully, her camera had been covered by her pashmina to avoid getting wet by the rain.

Realizing that the opportunity may never come again, Vaia snaps photos of every area deemed photo worthy. She stopped periodically to shelter from the rain.

As she lifted the camera one final time, Vaia felt an impact. A wave of anguish overwhelms her. She collided with one of the cyclists she'd seen in her earlier stroll.

"Mi scusi signorina, stai bene?" the collider spoke in Italian.

3

"Finally, brethren, whatsoever things are true, whatsoever things are honest, whatsoever things are just, whatsoever things are pure, whatsoever things are lovely, whatsoever things are of good report; if there be any virtue, and if there be any praise, think on these things." Philippians 4:8

Rubbing her knees and bruised ego, Vaia shakes her head. "I'm okay. Be careful next time. You're not the only one in the park."

Just then, two children approach them.

The boy looks up at the man. *"Padre, la signorina va bene?"*

"Go wait with your sister." The man turns his gaze back to Vaia. "Please miss, let me help you up."

"That's alright sir," Vaia declines, trying to ignore the whale sounds in her stomach. "I'm fine."

"I'm sorry that I bumped into you," the Italian man apologizes. "Where are you from?"

Thinking back to her Zeno escapade, she tried not to take notice of the man's obvious good looks. "*Lux Point Milano*, Starr Islands," Vaia whispers.

"I'm from Tuscany," he replies.

"Papa, I'm hungry," the girl cries.

"I'm sorry *signorina*, I must leave. Enjoy the rest of your visit. *Ciao bella*," he states, waving goodbye.

Of course he has children. His wife is probably somewhere in the park waiting for them. This trip is starting to become even more depressing. Is there ANY single man left on this planet?

Watching the man and his children walk off in the distance, Vaia sits on a nearby bench, hoping that no one had captured her unfortunate collision for social media.

In case she'd forgotten that she was hungry, her stomach whirred profusely. The fall made her head pound, so she slowly walked back to the *Piazza*.

Fifteen minutes later, Vaia notices a sign: *Gelateria Veneta Lucca*. Italian gelato would subdue hunger pangs until she returned to the ship.

Entering the quaint shop, Vaia inhales the coolness of the environment. Her eyes scan the kaleidoscope of gelato flavors. The cashier smiles warmly as she observes Vaia's awe.

"*Parla inglese?*" Vaia asks.

"*Si signorina*, I speak English," the woman nods.

The experience in the gelateria proved to be exactly what Vaia dreamed of: a wonderful exchange of beautiful language. Vaia picked up new words to add to her growing Italian vocabulary; perfect intonation and all.

The special of the day was five flavors for the price of one. Vaia chose Rocher, Banana, Cioccolato, Noce di Cocco, and Tiramisu. The flavors danced in her mouth like the musical notes from an orchestra; a symphony of excellence. Vaia took a mental note of the shop. This was definitely a place to revisit.

Just then, Vaia's phone vibrates in her purse. The sight of the number caused her eyes to twitch. It was her mother, Veria.

Hi my daughter. How is your trip?

Like clockwork Veria messaged. If a day went by and Vaia did not hear from her mother, she would contact law enforcement. It was that serious.

Although her mother was her favorite person in the world, she sometimes drove Vaia crazy.

Vaia's father died when she was a few months old, so she had no recollection of him. Veria chose not to remarry or speak about him. *'I cannot put myself through the emotional roller coaster of loving another man...'* her mother stated every time the topic came up. Who could blame her? Vaia understood all too well the pain of love and lost.

Hello mother. The trip is going well. I will share the details when I return.

Don't forget to smile. Let those men see your lovely face.

Vaia rolls her eyes as she contemplated how to respond to her mother, without being disrespectful.

What is it with this woman and my love life or lack thereof? Uggh!

When she arrived back on the ship, Vaia scrolled through the ship board calendar on the TV. Finally, she found something that appealed to her, *Singles Night Karaoke.*

After taking a shower and getting dressed, Vaia made her way down to the Singles Night venue. Though she did not care to highlight the obvious, she chose to savor the moment.

It was karaoke night and she decided to loosen up and take center stage. No one back home would believe her to do something so brave. Karaoke was about having fun, belting out your favorite tunes. No need to sound like a platinum recording artist.

Song choice:

Tears of Heartbreak by *Summer Zroledo*

Summer was Vaia's favorite artist. Known as the Queen of Breakup, Summer produced hit albums every year in Starr Islands.

Considering her wrecked emotional state, *Tears of Heartbreak* was not the song to choose after a recent breakup. However, Vaia let the painful melody pour out, connecting to every word of the song.

When Vaia finished, she received a standing ovation from the audience.

"Let's hear it for the pretty lady and her angelic voice," the karaoke host announced.

As Vaia made her way down the stage, her stomach signaled; food time.

Time for Quattro Formaggi pizza on the Lido Deck. Four cheese pizza. Yum...

The insides of her stomach jumped at the thought of authentic Italian pizza.

4

"To every thing there is a season, and a time to every purpose under the heaven..." Ecclesiastes 3:1

"*Signorina. Signorina,*" a man with a heavy Italian accent called out to Vaia. "Nice seeing you again. I did not get your name in the park."

Vaia turned around and spotted the collider waving at her. She smiled weakly and told him her name, "Vaia Bisenzo."

"I did not know you were a guest on this ship. Small world," he replies. "My name is Kalevi Náousa. These are my children Milos and Kaveri."

"Where is your wife?" Vaia blurts, flashing back again to the Athenaeum debacle.

"*La mamma è morta,*" Milos cries.

Kalevi covers his son's mouth. "My wife died two years ago."

"I am sorry," Vaia apologizes. "I did not mean to bring up such a sore topic."

"You did not know. It's alright." Kalevi smiles at her. "Join us," he motions.

"Oh no," Vaia declines, "I cannot interrupt your family time."

"I invited you to join us. It's not an interruption."

Kaveri grabs Vaia's hand and pulls her to their table. "You're pretty. Pretty ladies sit at this table."

"Okay," Vaia nods. "But only for a few minutes."

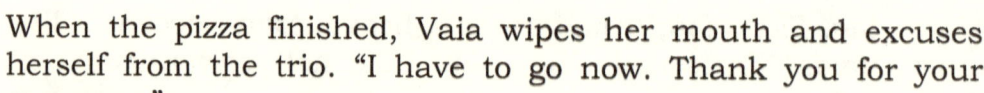

When the pizza finished, Vaia wipes her mouth and excuses herself from the trio. "I have to go now. Thank you for your company."

"Byeeee *signorina*," the children sing in unison.

Kalevi stands up and waves to her. "*Buona notte signorina. Sogni d'oro*. Sweet dreams."

As Vaia walked away, a smile plastered over her face. *Wow, okay then. I see that the good looking men are in Italy. Vaia stop it. That man does not want you...*

"He healeth the broken in heart, and bindeth up their wounds." Psalm 147:3

1 AM

Vaia decided to scroll through her phone reminiscing on the good times she had with her ex, contemplating why she chose to end their relationship.

What am I doing? He chose work over me.

For the four years they'd dated, her ex was attentive **only** when they were face to face. For him it was truly *out of sight out of mind*. Not quite the feeling one wanted to have as a future wife.

The day she ended things, he replied nonchalantly. *'There's nothing here for me. I'm going back to my country...'* That response pierced her heart, since it was a decision clearly made without her.

Staring at the final picture, Vaia exhales.

"This is ridiculous. He isn't even thinking about me. Why am I torturing myself?"

"The best way to get over someone... delete their very existence," Vaia once heard Summer Zroledo say in an interview.

Taking Summer's advice, Vaia begins to delete all of the videos, photos, and texts that connected her to the man who broke her heart. She even cleared her call log. No more allowing a mere human to suck her energy. She was someone who enjoyed her own company.

"It's time to make moves."

On her knees crying out to Jesus, was Vaia's go to remedy for any negative situation. It had been four months since her baptism. She learned that Jesus Christ truly loved her and could fill the voids in her life.

After her prayer, Vaia closed her eyes and entered dreamland.

6

"Who can find a virtuous woman? for her price is far above rubies." Proverbs 31:10

The cruise director runs on stage in an eccentric heart covered suit, announcing the beginning of the Marriage Game Show.

Once the three couples were chosen, Vaia watched intently as the show proceeded. Moments later, Kalevi walks into the venue with a drink in his hand.

It took everything inside her not to call out to him like a girl with a crush. Though the lights were dim, Vaia could still recognize Kalevi.

A random burst of adrenaline shocks her and she bolts out of the lounge to catch her breath.

"Miss, is everything ok?"

Vaia looks up to see a concerned waiter standing next to her.

"I'm okay," she nods. "Thank you."

25 Becoming a Royal Princess

"You look pale. I can take you to the medical center," the man replies. "It's no problem."

"Chocolate gets pale?" she grunts.

"I do not understand, miss."

"It means I'm fine. Thanks again." Vaia knew that race was a heated topic and inappropriate to bring up given their current location.

Vaia enters the elevator, fanning herself. Although she ate pizza with Kalevi the night before, it wasn't a date.

Inside her room, she begins to exhale profusely.

What's wrong with me? I can't be thinking about Kalevi. I don't even know him. He probably has a wife. Oh wait, he's a widower. Why do I care? Vaia, SNAP OUT OF IT! That man is not thinking about you.

Vaia looked in the mirror and noted her flushed face. Something was off. This experience was new. Her thoughts flooded with possibilities of a relationship with the stranger. She had to lie down.

"For I know the thoughts that I think toward you, saith the Lord, thoughts of peace, and not of evil, to give you an expected end." Jeremiah 29:11

It had been days since Vaia saw Kalevi at the game show. She made it her objective to evade all on board activities and eating meals in the dining areas; opting instead to order room service for every meal.

This was not how she intended to end her vacation: running from a man who probably had zero interest in her. Clearly she needed a cruise do over in the near future.

She decided to put on her elegant dress for the final night: **Captain's Night**. Too bad she'd be dining alone. Although she could've avoided the fuss and sheer embarrassment, Vaia felt a strong urge to attend the final dinner on the ship.

"Can I take your order, miss?" the waiter asks, waiting for Vaia to decide.

She hands the man her menu. "I'll have the *Quayap Soup* and *Chicken Brisk*."

"Great choice."

"Food from my country," she proudly announces.

Hopefully it tastes like home...

The waiter smiles. "Your food will be out shortly."

It was the final night of the cruise and Kalevi was eager to enjoy the time with his children. As they walked into the restaurant, his son calls out, "Papa, it's *signorina* Vaia. Let's go say hi."

Kalevi tries to hide his excitement seeing the woman who caught his attention at the park. He felt a tad bit guilty for looking at any woman who was not Sivõrï, his wife. Though widowed for two years, he wasn't ready to love another. However, something about Vaia piqued his interest. For the past week, his children had been playing a daily game of '*Who could find signorina?*'

Aside from the night he spotted her at the Marriage Game Show, tonight was the first time any of them had seen her. Fear overtook him and he opted not to approach her before she left the venue in haste.

He recalled how beautiful she'd looked in her tightly coiled hair, no make-up, and flowy A-line dress. He loved looking at her *dulce de leche* skin. To put it in simple words, Vaia looked good without effort.

Kalevi fought daily with his feelings. *A woman as beautiful as Vaia is probably married.*

"Let's not disturb her—" Before he could finish the sentence, his children joined Vaia at her table.

"Hi *signorina*," Milos and Kaveri greets.

"Can we sit with you? We have been looking everywhere for you," Milos utters.

"You have?" Vaia glances at Kalevi.

"Yes, we thought you were hurt or worse," Milos gasps.

"I'm sorry to have scared you, little ones," Vaia replies.

"Why do you look sad?"

Vaia looks at the girl. "I'm not sad, Kaveri."

"You need gelato. Whenever papa wants to cheer us up he gives us gelato." Kalevi's daughter calls out to a waiter, "Excuse me waiter, can you please bring *signorina* a chocolate gelato? She is sad."

The waiter smiles. "Of course little miss."

Kalevi stares at his children and then grins nervously at Vaia. "I'm sorry for all of this. They're just excited to see you."

"They're not bothering me," Vaia chuckles. "I love children."

"Papa, can we go see the aquarium over there?" Kaveri asks.

29 Becoming a Royal Princess

"Stay where I can see you," Kalevi says.

Kaveri claps excitedly. "Let's go brother."

"I'm coming," Milos answers.

Kalevi turns his gaze to Vaia. The clock ticked as the question danced in his mind. Gathering up the courage he slowly asks, "Do you and your **husband** have any children?"

Vaia shakes her head, noting the man's apprehension. "I'm not married. My students are my children."

"Aren't you too young to be a teacher?"

"Just how young do you think I am?"

"I don't know," he shrugs. "Most teachers I know have gray hair."

"I started teaching when I was 22."

"Last year?"

"Are you trying to flirt?"

"Is it working?" Kalevi winks.

"I'm 30 years old since you're afraid to ask," Vaia giggles. "How old are you?"

"32. Milos is 8. Kaveri is 7."

At that moment the atmosphere was calm for both Vaia and Kalevi.

"This is the final day of our cruise, are you happy to go back home?" Vaia inquires.

"I would've been happier if I got to see you more, now that I know you're single," he laughs. "I will miss you."

"You don't even know me," she quips, avoiding staring into his green eyes; she hadn't noticed the color before.

Pay attention Vaia, pay attention...

"Let's end dinner early, shall we?" Kalevi interrupts her thoughts. "I will put the children in camp so that we can speak freely. Meet me in ten minutes near the spa entrance."

He can't be serious. Wait, he's serious?

"There is no fear in love; but perfect love casteth out fear..."
1 John 4:18

Vaia throws herself on the bed; a million questions dancing around her head. Who was this man? Could she trust him?

She looked in the mirror, deciding on whether to change. Her suitcase was filled with unused garments.

I don't have time for one night flings. What do I know about this man? Am I really going on a fake date with him? This is unlike me.

Five minutes later, against her better judgment, Vaia makes her way to the 12th floor. What was the worst that could happen on a ship with numerous cameras and workers? If she felt uncomfortable, she had two choices: run or scream.

Kalevi exits the elevator and wipes beads of sweat from his forehead. He couldn't recall the last time he was nervous around a woman.

You can do this Kalevi. She's just a pretty lady. You can do this.

Mustering up all his courage, Kalevi walks to the spa entrance and sees Vaia standing there. "We meet again," he greets.

"It isn't a surprise since you set this up," Vaia chuckles.

"I didn't want to tell you this in front of my children, but you are beautiful beyond words. Like a queen."

Vaia holds up her hand in contention. "You seem like a nice man and father, but flings aren't something I do. Let's save all the getting to know you talk for those we are truly meant to be with."

"Who is to say that we aren't speaking to each other at this very moment?"

Vaia gulps. "Before we start something that will go nowhere, I'm going to call it a night. It was a pleasure meeting you Kalevi. Safe travels back home."

"What are you afraid of?" he counters.

"I'm not afraid. I just can't do this again. My last relationship was a waste of four years. You seem to have experienced great love and have two wonderful children. I hope you find what you're looking for. But, I can assure you that it's certainly not with me," Vaia says. "Goodbye."

Watching Vaia head down the stairs, Kalevi smiles to himself. *Wow, she's truly something. Got my work cut out for me. This I like.*

9

"If any of you lack wisdom, let him ask of God..." James 1:5

Two days passed since Vaia's encounter with Kalevi. As the jetlag wore off, a wave of disappointment took its place when she realized she'd spent ten days on a cruise and had only one day worth of photos as proof of her vacation. After logging into her account, she typed a few words into the search engine.

🔍 Cruises to Europe

What she did not expect was a notification for an **Avenami** friend request from *Kalevi Náousa*. It seemed as though he'd searched for her. She was more creeped out than flattered. What if he turned out to be a stalker or worse?

Her fingers clearly had a mind of its own because she found herself clicking the Accept button.

When she opened her account, her notification pinged with a message from Kalevi.

Vaia paced her bedroom as she contemplated whether or not to respond to his message. After her last disaster of a relationship, she was in no mood to waste any more time entertaining men and their *alleged* interest in her.

After what seemed like an eternity, she decided to open the message. If she didn't like it, she'd delete it.

> *Buongiorno signorina Vaia. I cannot stop thinking about you. I want to have an actual conversation with you. I want to hear your voice again. I hope you respond to this message. We can set up our first call or video chat. Ciao.*

She didn't know why Kalevi's message made her smile. Clicking the reply button, she proceeded to respond. However, her cell phone rang and cut off the reply.

"Well, I see that you're alive," Veria shrieked over the phone. "Why didn't you call to let me know that you've arrived safely? You ignored my texts."

"Sorry mom. I've been dealing with jetlag," Vaia exhales.

"Save your excuses."

"I don't have the energy for this," Vaia says, rolling her eyes.

"Did you meet anyone?" Veria asks, ignoring her daughter's annoyance.

"Sort of..."

"I'll be right over."

"NO! I need my rest."

"You can rest AFTER you give me grandbabies," Veria retorts, hanging up the phone.

10

"There is neither Jew nor Greek, there is neither bond nor free, there is neither male nor female: for ye are all one in Christ Jesus." Galatians 3:28

The noise emanating from Veria's arrival was obvious. She rang the doorbell nonstop until Vaia opened.

"Hi mom," Vaia mumbles, when she opens the door.

"You look good baby," Veria greets with air kisses.

"Really?" Vaia groans. "I'm exhausted."

"Do you want me to make *Cobalt Tea*?"

"Help yourself, I don't want anything," she declines, as they walked towards the kitchen.

Veria pulls out a kitchen stool to sit. "Tell me about the man you 'sort of' met."

"That's all you care about?"

"You're my only daughter. What are you waiting for? Your younger brother's already married."

"That's great for him. You know that I just ended my engagement."

"That was **months** ago. I didn't like him for you. Wasted too much of your time. If you'd listen to me from the start—"

"Okayyyyy mother," Vaia stresses.

"Back to Mr. S.O."

"That's not his name. Is this conversation even relevant? I just want to sleep."

"Spill," Veria demands.

"Can we talk about this tomorrow?"

"Time is of the essence, child. I want to hear about this man."

Vaia exhales the frustration bubbling on the inside and gave in to her mother's request. "His name is Kalevi Náousa from Tuscany. He's 32. Widowed with one son and one daughter," she reveals, showing Veria his picture.

"Of all the men in the world you pick a widower with *two children*?" Veria replies in disdain. "That's the best you could do? Used goods?" she scoffs.

"Why are you being so critical? I don't even like him."

"And to top it off he's a *vanilla*?"

"You know that I don't care about race. We're all humans."

"I don't want you to get hurt. Chocolate and vanilla don't mix. Didn't you learn from the last time?"

"We're not in the 1900s. In this century, you marry who you love. Skin complexion is irrelevant."

"What does he do for a living?" Veria continues.

"We did not discuss his work," Vaia replies.

"What if he's broke and trying to marry his way into Starr Islands to improve his status? What if you enter into a relationship and he leaves you like Easton did?"

"Stop being negative, Kalevi and I aren't in a relationship," Vaia responds. "We only spoke a few times. It's really not that big of a deal. I just think he's good looking, that's all."

"End it before it begins," Veria snaps. "I can't see you get hurt again."

"I won't."

"Get ready. We're going shopping."

"I don't wanna," Vaia moans.

"You're too old to whine. Stop that. You have five minutes."

I wonder if any other daughters are pressured about marriage. What time is it? I'm tired.

11

"So God created man in his own image, in the image of God created he him; male and female created he them."
Genesis 1:27

Lucca, Italy

Kalevi greets his mother. "How was your trip?"

"Business as usual, no pleasure," she scoffs. "But you, you look different. I can't quite put my finger on it."

"How do I look?"

"Figlio mio, sembri molto felice."

"I'm always happy," Kalevi replies.

"This is different. You had the same look when you first met Sivõrï—" Kavala gasps, "Did you meet a woman?"

Kalevi nods. "I did."

"Why did you keep this information from me?"

"I'm still processing it."

"Well, don't keep me in suspense. Who is she? Where is she from? What does she do? Did she meet the children?"

"Her name is Vaia Bisenzo from *Lux Point Milano*. She's a teacher. Yes, she met the children and they love her," Kalevi shares, excitedly.

"This is amazing," Kavala peers over her son's shoulder. "Can I see a picture?"

"I sent her an **Avenami** friend request. Let me see if she responded." Kalevi opens his laptop and smiles when he sees Vaia's acceptance of his request. He shows his mother Vaia's picture.

"I don't like her," Kavala replies, twitching.

"Why?"

"She's uh— She does not look like us," Kavala blurts. "No. I do not approve."

Kalevi looks at his mother. "This is not your decision to make."

"What will people say? You are the Crown Prince of Lucca; a very wealthy man. Who you marry affects a lot of people. You know this already."

"Actually, it only affects me and my children. We are all God's creation," Kalevi states, walking to the window.

"ENOUGH with your religious talk," Kavala scolds. "You will bring no woman who looks like **her** on these grounds. Do you understand?"

"*A woman who looks like **her**?* What does that mean?"

"You know exactly what I mean. Forget about that woman, do you hear me?"

"No mother, I don't. Now if you'll excuse me—"

"Don't speak to me like that," Kavala snaps.

"I'm going to the kitchen," Kalevi replies, excusing himself from the toxicity of his mother's words.

12

"And let us not be weary in well doing: for in due season we shall reap, if we faint not." Galatians 6:9

One Week Later

Kalevi enters the palace overwhelmed; his meeting with the Members of Parliament was daunting. As a Christian, many of their policies didn't line up with his values, but he knew it was his duty to ensure that all citizens lived peacefully.

The changes would be a matter of prayer and fasting. He knew that with God, anything was possible. However, the leaders of the Parliament had an issue with his marital status.

He explained that marriage was important to him and he had to choose the right wife. This caused an uproar, with many of the members stating that the *women of Lucca were suitable candidates*. No one cared about his religious beliefs in choosing a *godly wife*.

As he walked through the palace, he uttered a prayer.

God, please give me the strength to endure the criticism and everything that comes with being a leader. I know You have the best in store for me and I do not want to step out of Your will.

His plan for the afternoon was to spend much needed time resting. The pain in his temples proved immense.

As customary, he entered his children's playroom to ask about their day. Once inside, he notices Kaveri comforting a tearful Milos.

Kalevi goes to console his son. "Milos, why are you crying?"

"Papa," the boy sobs, "when is *mamma* coming back?"

"Your *mamma's* in a better place."

"What's better than the palace?" Milos replies.

"Heaven."

"She's never coming back?" Milos continues crying. "I'm not going to see her again?"

The pain in his son's eyes pricked Kalevi's heart. Kalevi hugs Milos. "You will see her again when you get to heaven. For now, your *mamma* will always be a part of you. She loves you. We both love you."

"If she loved me she wouldn't have died," Milos pouts.

"I'm here," Kalevi offers.

"I want *mio mamma*. All of my friends have their mothers. Our family is incomplete," Milos sighs.

"Whoa," Kalevi replies. "Where'd you learn that?"

"In class we were taught that all families have a mother, father, and children. This family only has a father, children, and *Nonna*."

"Then that's our family," Kalevi explains. "Not all families are the same, but what we all share is love. I love you. Kaveri loves you. *Nonna* loves you. Most of all, God loves you."

Milos wipes his tears. "Can I get a new *mamma*?"

"What do you mean?"

"Get married, papa. Isn't that how *le madri* become *madri*, by marrying *padri*?" Milos asks, innocently.

"I'll have to explain it to you again, but you're on the right track; marriage first. **Always** remember that." He turns to his daughter. "Kaveri how was your day? Are you ready for your tea party?"

"Yes. Can we get gelato? I'm exhausted from brother's crying." Kaveri fans herself dramatically. "I need cheering up."

"Where are you two learning to speak like this? What do you know about being exhausted?" Kalevi asks, amused.

Kaveri giggles. *"Papà, sei divertente."*

"You think I'm funny? You think I'm funny?" he asks, scooping up his daughter. "Let's go get a snack." He turns to Milos. "You coming?"

Milos nods and follows his father and sister out of the room.

13

"And now abideth faith, hope, charity, these three; but the greatest of these is charity." 1 Corinthians 13:13

After spending time with his children, Kalevi strolls to his study.

Kavala stops his gait. "Why the morose look? How was the meeting?"

"Challenging," he laments. "I've never had opposition this intense. My marital status is causing quite an uproar."

"Being married is important in our monarchy. It's part of the tradition. All princes in our family have been married men."

"I'm a widower."

"For two long years. Don't you think it's time you moved on?"

"I'm ready to—"

Kavala holds up her finger in contention and shakes her head. "I hope you're not referring to that woman."

"Her name is Vaia," Kalevi smiles.

"She isn't a part of our culture and she's a *donna di colore*."

"Irrelevant," Kalevi retorts. "Italy is multiracial and we're all one under God."

"Oh come off it," Kavala scoffs. "We've never had a colored member in the House of Náousa."

"It troubles me that people are still judging others by the color of their skin, when we're all humans. That's the **only** race."

"Tradition is tradition," Kavala sings. "No need to change it. There are many beautiful single women in Lucca, why do you have to choose one from this Starr Islands place?"

"I don't know what will happen between Vaia and me, but I'm starting to have strong feelings for her."

"I will find a suitable wife for you from LUCCA who looks like us."

"I'm capable of finding my own wife."

"We'll speak about this later," his mother snaps.

"There's nothing further to discuss. It's my decision."

14

"Be not deceived: evil communications corrupt good manners."
1 Corinthians 15:33

Vaia thought long and hard about what her mother said the previous week. Though skin color didn't matter to her, the difference in culture might be a cause for concern. What did she know about Italian men? What if she wasn't accepted into their society? Yes, the world was filled with interracial couples and children, but that didn't mean everyone accepted it.

She'd never told her mother, but that was an early challenge with her ex, Easton; the stares that she received whenever they traveled together. Not particularly in Starr Islands, but other countries.

What made her think it'd be different with Kalevi? *Lux Point Milano* was a country filled with interracial couples, so no one looked twice at them.

This is drama I do not need. I know who I am in Christ so I am going to wait for whoever God sends my way. I can't bombard my thoughts with negativity. Love is love and whoever God has for me must first love Jesus and everything else will fall into place. God created us all EQUAL!

Just then her phone pinged. It was a message from her mother...

Vaia was in no mood for any surprises.

An hour later, Veria enters Vaia's house frantically. "Why aren't you dressed?"

"What is this about, mom?"

"You have a date."

"Excuse me?" Vaia grumbles. "What date?"

"I signed you up for an online dating website."

"MOM!" she yells. "Why would you do that?"

"You need to get married," Veria states, nonchalantly.

"I don't need your help."

"Yes you do," Veria nods. "You've been wallowing in gloom for almost a year over that stupid man."

"No I haven't. Why did you put my business on the internet? You know I am a private person."

"I didn't put much, just the basics. And you've had hundreds of likes and messages from some great candidates."

"I don't care. I'm not interested," Vaia contends.

"Well then I guess you'll have to tell him for yourself." Veria points to the door.

"Tell who?"

"Your date, he'll be here in a few minutes."

Vaia shakes her head. "You can't be serious."

"I am. So **get dressed!**"

15

"Can two walk together, except they be agreed?" Amos 3:3

When the doorbell rang, Vaia felt uneasiness in the pit of her stomach. She didn't want to go the online route of finding love. And she certainly didn't want her mother's assistance. However, she decided to give it a try since it was something she'd never done before. The thirties was a new decade. No more living in fear.

"He's here," Veria announces excitedly.

"I don't know why you're smiling. Have you even met this man before?"

"No, but his stats seems up your alley."

"Is he a Christian?" Vaia wonders.

"He listed *religious* under his status."

"That's not an answer."

"Well ask him yourself," Veria replies casually. "He's educated, has a career, his own house, car, and he's an avid traveler. What more do you want?"

"This seems like a bad idea," Vaia sighs.

"How do you expect to find love if you don't go out and meet men? Clearly there are no men at your job. You've stated that there are no single men at the church you attend, so... Online dating it is."

"It doesn't feel right."

Veria pulls her daughter to the door. "You're a grown woman honey; I believe that you can handle whatever comes your way. As I said, his stats seem legit."

"You need to show this much interest in finding love for yourself. I want a stepfather."

"This is about you Vaia," Veria contends. "Let's not keep the young man waiting."

Vaia shakes her head. "You're always dodging the topic."

"Come in," Veria greets Vaia's date, moments later.

"I was beginning to think that I wasn't welcomed."

You're not.

"I've been ringing the bell for five minutes," the man jokes. "Hello Vaia."

Vaia wrinkles her nose. "And your name is?"

"Don't you know my name from our conversations?" he inquires.

"Sorry to burst your bubble, but I didn't set up any date with you, it was my mother." She glances at Veria.

The man's eyes widen. "Your mother?"

"That will be me. My name is Veria," she says.

"This is quite awkward," Vaia's date mumbles.

"It's okay young man. My daughter needs love in her life and I took it upon myself to help her."

Vaia rolls her eyes.

"It's alright. A story to tell our children," he chuckles.

"Children?" Vaia scoffs. "I don't even know your name."

"See," Veria grins. "I like him already. He's talking about children."

"Mom, would you stop?" Vaia turns back to her date. "Your name?"

He hands her a bouquet of flowers. "These are for you by the way."

Vaia takes the bouquet and hands it to her mother. "Thanks. Your name?" she repeats.

"My name's Kolb Ticofan."

"*Vaia Ticofan.* Has a nice ring to it, don't you think, sweetie?" her mother chuckles.

Vaia shoots her mother a ferocious glare as she exited the house with Kolb.

"See you later," her mother smiles, closing in the door. "I see potential from this date…"

16

"Flee also youthful lusts..." 2 Timothy 2:22

When they arrive at the restaurant ten minutes later, to Vaia's amazement it was a five star restaurant; the type of establishment that you read about on food blogs.

"Ticofan, party of two," Kolb announces at the front desk.

"Right this way sir," the waitress escorts.

At their table, Kolb pulls out the chair for Vaia to have a seat.

This doesn't seem so bad. Okay. I can do this. He's already starting off on the right foot.

"Thanks," she grins.

"You look **hot** by the way." Kolb takes a sip of his water and gurgles.

*And **there** it goes. I knew it was too good to be true...*

"Excuse me?" Vaia answers. She was repulsed by his atrocious table manners; it was a shift from his previous kind gesture.

"Your picture didn't do you justice," Kolb continues with lust in his eyes.

"Are you ready to order?" the waitress asks them.

"Wow, aren't you a pretty number," Kolb whistles, at the waitress. "I'll have a *Breaded Hazelnut Pork, Miomei Pasta, Whipped Coriander Flatbread* and a glass of your finest wine."

The waitress turns to Vaia. "And for you, miss?"

"I'll just have the *Anise Duck Stew* with a *Parchese Salad* and a glass of *Sparkling Passion Fruit Cider,*" Vaia replies, still in shock.

"I will be back with your order shortly," the waitress states, walking away in disgust.

Kolb turns his gaze from checking out the waitress and grins at Vaia. "How long do you think you'll be a teacher?"

Vaia tried to practice self-control, taking deep breaths as she eyed her date. "I don't understand."

"That's not a profession that brings in the, you know, **bacon**... Lemme spell it out for you, teaching is a noble profession, don't get me wrong, but they don't get paid as much as they should. I need to be with someone who is financially solid," he derides.

"I love what I do for a living. I get to educate the future leaders of our nations."

Kolb laughs out loud. "Cliché response. How many children do you want? I want to have two. Any more than that and my wife's body would be ugly."

Vaia stares at Kolb. "Is this seriously how you communicate with women?"

"I speak my mind," he shrugs. "Nothing's wrong with confidence."

"This is a first date and you're ogling another woman in front of me. Even the waitress looked mortified."

"She's pretty. Are you one of those insecure types?"

"Do you hear yourself?"

"Loud and clear," Kolb grins. "I love the sound of my voice. I want to be an actor."

"What is it that you do, *now*?"

"I'm *in between jobs*."

"According to my mom, your profile description says that you're *educated with a career, your own house, car, and an avid traveler*," Vaia regurgitates.

"I see you've memorized my stats." He takes another sip of his water. "Of course I lied. Everyone lies online. Even setting up this date, it was your mom. But, I forgive her because you're hot," Kolb laughs.

Vaia plays with her napkin, debating whether or not she should run out of the restaurant. "None of it is true?"

"Well... I am educated, got my High School diploma. My career is still in the works. I share an apartment with my friends. I'm waiting for my parents to kick the bucket so I can get their house. Can't have my wife living with the in-laws, you know," he shrugs. "Let me see, what else? Oh yes, I take public transportation. Why waste money on gas and insurance? I borrowed the car we drove in tonight. A mere investment I hope you'll pay for later. I travel to various destinations in the city," Kolb explains.

"There should be a law against dating profilers who waste people's time," she snaps.

"Putting all that aside," Kolb continues, "let's just cut to the chase; I'm not interested in a relationship at the moment."

"What exactly is it that you're interested in then, Mr. Ticofan?"

Kolb looks at her lustfully. "I've arranged for us to go to a hotel room after this if you're up for it," he winks.

Vaia picks up her belongings and runs out of the restaurant.

"Where are you going?" Kolb screams after her. "I have protection—"

Vaia enters her house panting. She headed straight to the shower to hopefully wash off the filth of her atrocious date. She ignores the urge to answer the phone ringing on her dresser as the water splashed on her face.

Uggh! I don't want to speak to anyone right now...

Thirty minutes later, the doorbell rang. Clearly her mother didn't get the memo: she didn't want to be bothered.

"Why didn't you answer my calls?" Veria barges in. "I thought something happened to you."

"It's 11:50PM, why are you here so late?"

"I came to check up on you. You didn't call me after your date or answer my calls. I almost called the police."

"I'm not missing. Besides, I'm an adult; I don't need you to rescue me."

"A mother shouldn't be concerned for her child because she's an **adult**?"

"I just want to go to bed," Vaia mumbles. "Are you staying the night? The guest bedroom's ready if you need it."

"Don't dismiss me like that," Veria calls out to her daughter heading up the stairs. "I want to hear about your date."

Vaia stops mid ascent. "Listen to me clearly, mother. I do not want you to EVER help me when it comes to my love life, do you hear me?"

"What happened? I sense anger in your voice," Veria replies, innocently.

"Kolb is a liar. Nothing he said on his profile is true. He's a deadbeat."

"So what if he embellished his status a little? Everyone does it. No one wants to paint themselves in a negative light."

Vaia reaches the top of the staircase. "Whaaaatttt?"

"How did it go?"

Vaia begins to huff angrily.

"What happened, sweetie?"

Holding her temples, Vaia reveals the details of her awful date. "He started the date by flirting with the waitress and then he made offensive comments about the female post-pregnancy body. His speech was abysmal. If all that wasn't bad enough, he asked me if I wanted to go to a hotel after our date. And I'm sure it wasn't for a *Bible Study*, since he's so *religious*."

Veria gasps. "Vaia, I'm sorry. As much as I want you to get married, I don't want you with a man who degrades women. That date sounds disastrous."

"Take my profile off of that site and avoid trying to hook me up with anyone in the future. Leave the matchmaking to Jesus."

17

"Seek the Lord and his strength, seek his face continually."
1 Chronicles 16:11

A few days later, Vaia turned on her laptop and saw notifications from one Mr. Kalevi Náousa. Most of the messages he'd ask about her day.

They hadn't spoken to one another after she initially accepted his friend request. Social media wasn't something she used often, but today she felt inclined to check it.

The end of May meant school closings. She now had time to go online. Vaia opens a new message box and began to type.

Hi Kalevi, this is Vaia. I hope that all is well with you and your children. Have a great day.

He responded immediately.

Was he online waiting for her?

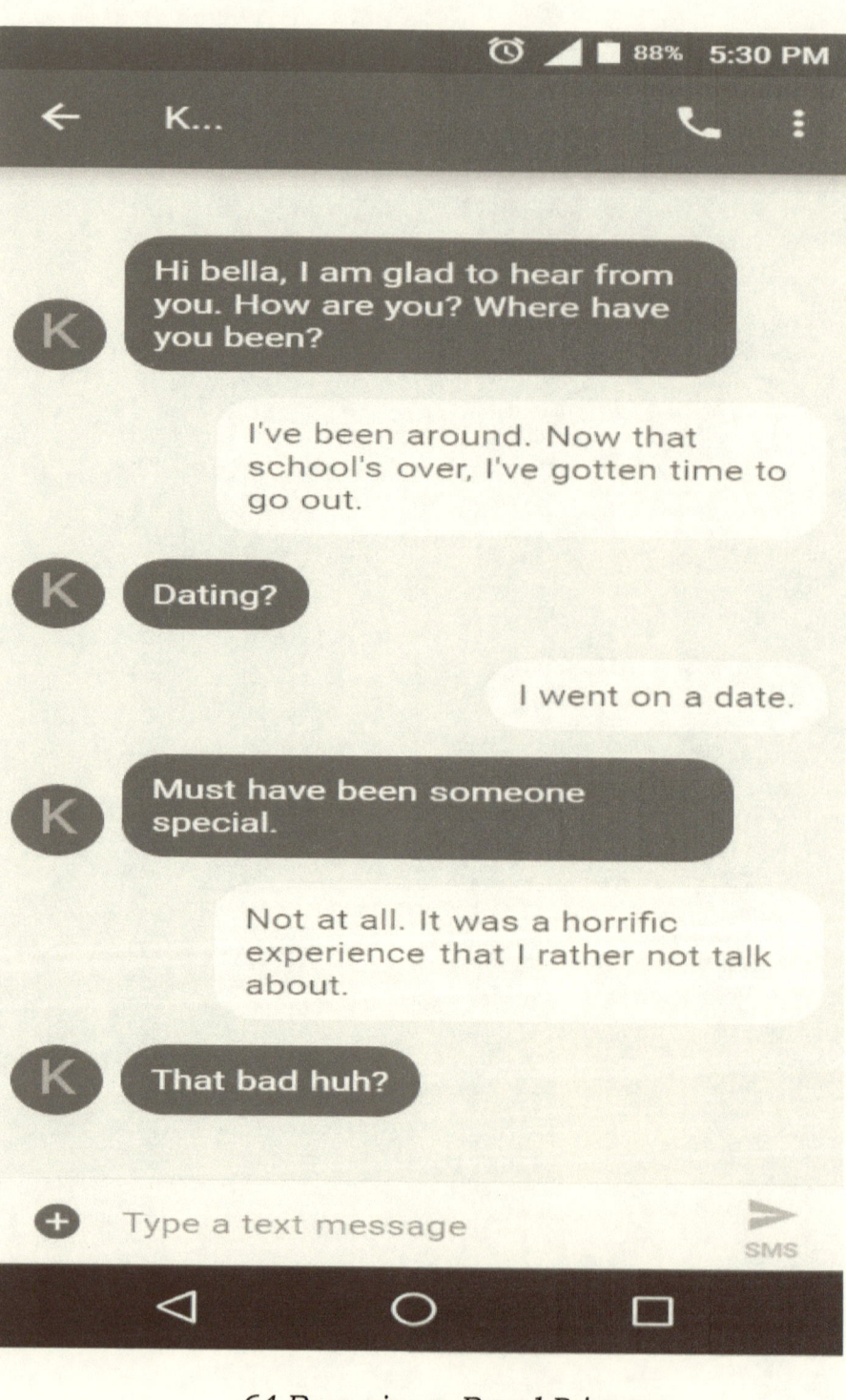

K: Hi bella, I am glad to hear from you. How are you? Where have you been?

I've been around. Now that school's over, I've gotten time to go out.

K: Dating?

I went on a date.

K: Must have been someone special.

Not at all. It was a horrific experience that I rather not talk about.

K: That bad huh?

Type a text message

SMS

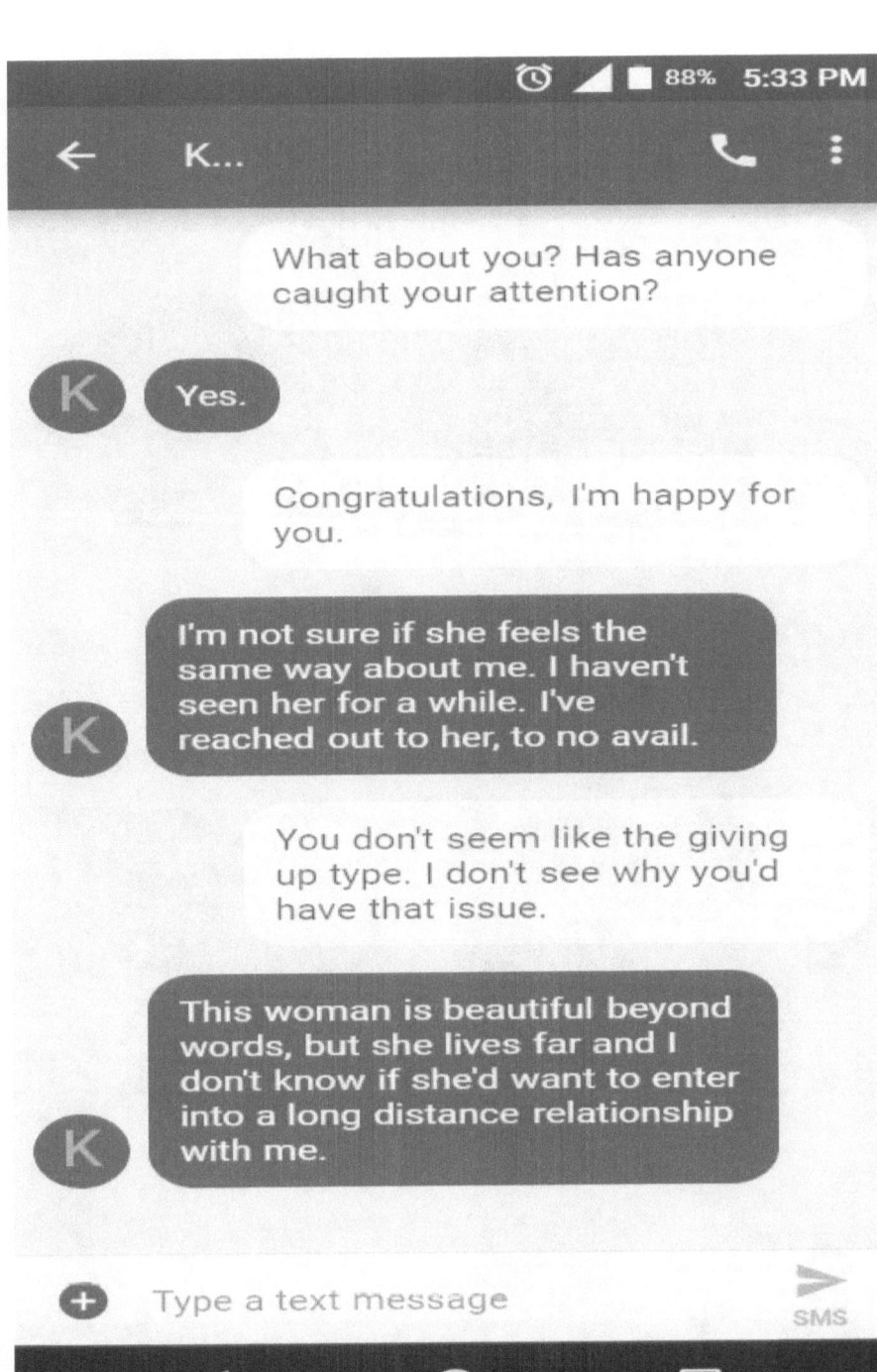

What about you? Has anyone caught your attention?

K Yes.

Congratulations, I'm happy for you.

K I'm not sure if she feels the same way about me. I haven't seen her for a while. I've reached out to her, to no avail.

You don't seem like the giving up type. I don't see why you'd have that issue.

K This woman is beautiful beyond words, but she lives far and I don't know if she'd want to enter into a long distance relationship with me.

Type a text message

SMS

65 Becoming a Royal Princess

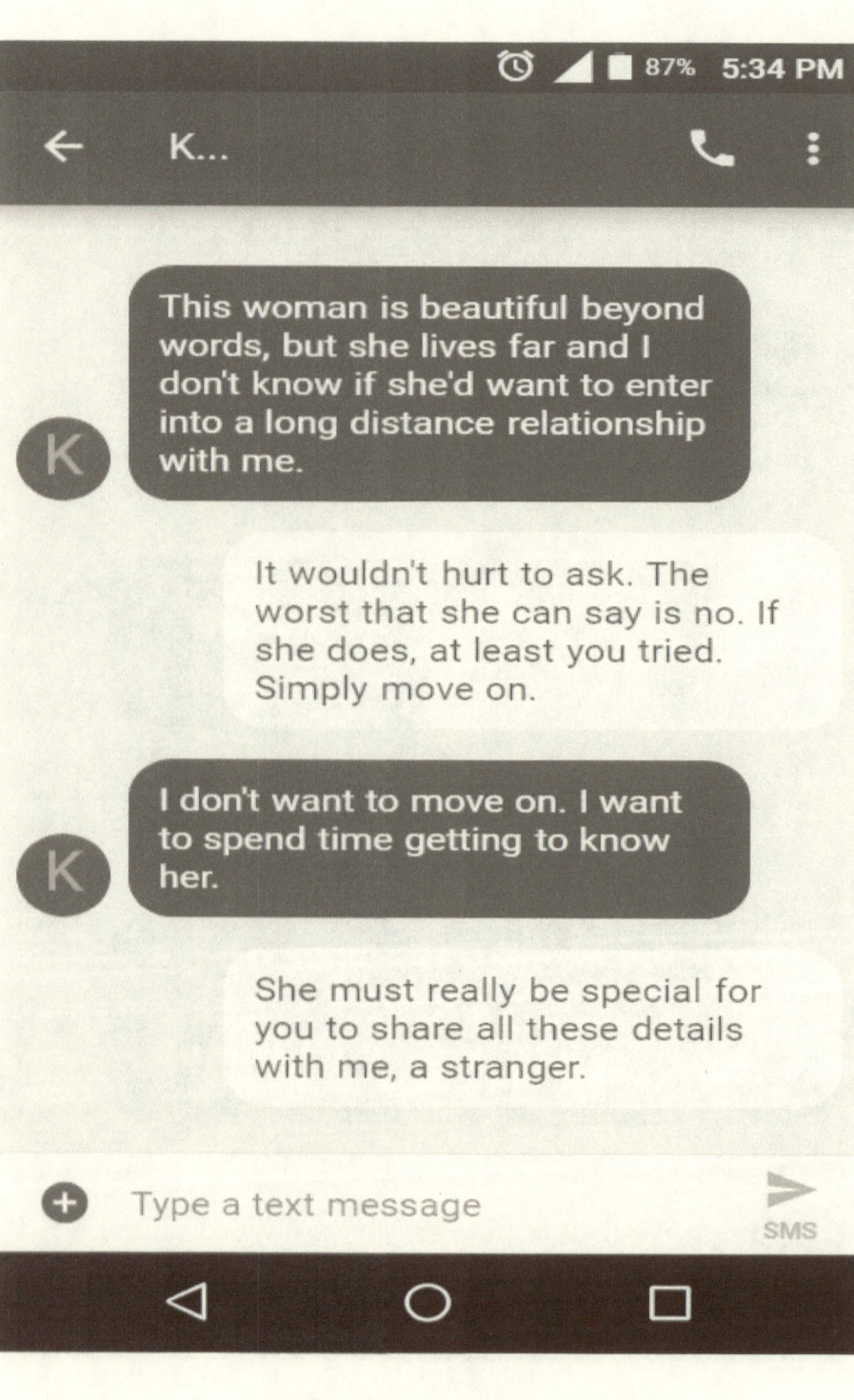

K

This woman is beautiful beyond words, but she lives far and I don't know if she'd want to enter into a long distance relationship with me.

It wouldn't hurt to ask. The worst that she can say is no. If she does, at least you tried. Simply move on.

K

I don't want to move on. I want to spend time getting to know her.

She must really be special for you to share all these details with me, a stranger.

Type a text message

SMS

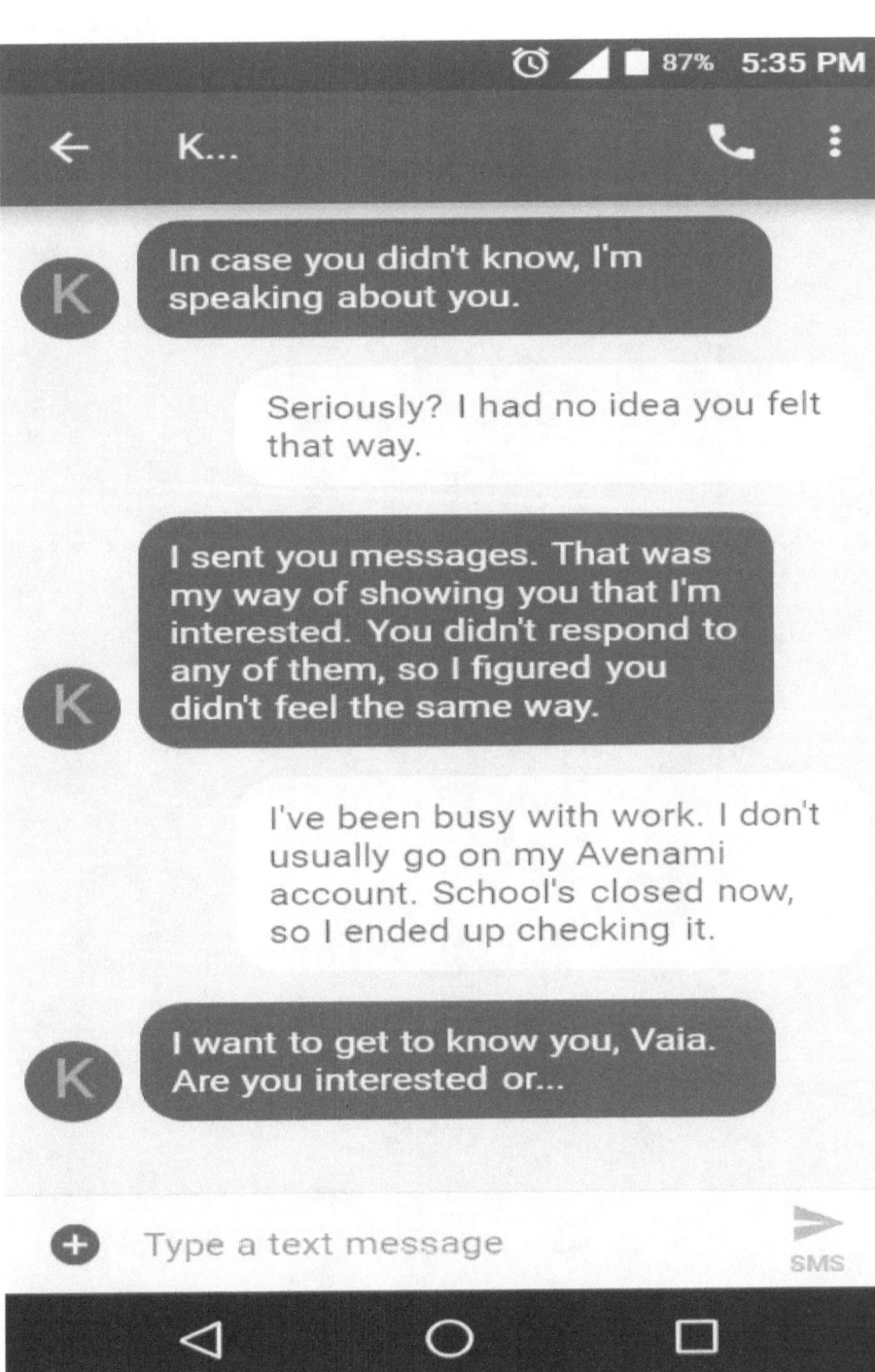

K In case you didn't know, I'm speaking about you.

Seriously? I had no idea you felt that way.

K I sent you messages. That was my way of showing you that I'm interested. You didn't respond to any of them, so I figured you didn't feel the same way.

I've been busy with work. I don't usually go on my Avenami account. School's closed now, so I ended up checking it.

K I want to get to know you, Vaia. Are you interested or...

Type a text message

SMS

Vaia stares at the screen in shock.

Mr. Gorgeous Italian collider himself, is interested in **ME**? *As in me? Vaia? Is this a joke?*

18

"But seek ye first the kingdom of God, and his righteousness; and all these things shall be added unto you." Matthew 6:33

Two Months Later

Even with the time difference, Vaia and Kalevi managed to make it a priority to have meaningful conversations. They shared much of their lives with one another and Vaia detested ending their calls. Kalevi was everything she prayed for and more in a husband.

"Come back to Italy," Kalevi utters.

It was the one request she evaded the numerous times he asked. She couldn't bring herself to say yes. It still seemed too soon. During their initial phone call, he made it clear that he was not interested in dating. He wanted a wife.

She'd agreed with his request to ask God's permission before beginning any deep conversations. They'd both gotten the confirmation they needed and began their courtship.

However, there was something about him that Vaia could not figure out. A major part of him he had not shared; his job, or perhaps, lack thereof. She'd resisted the urge to do an extensive search for him online. Since privacy was an important part of how she lived her life, she didn't want to invade anyone else's. The last thing she needed was to financially care for a grown man and his children. She'd heard many stories of single women being duped for their money. And she definitely didn't want to be a victim of fraud.

Conversing with Vaia had been more exciting than any Kalevi had since his wife died. Many women wanted to be the next Mrs. Náousa because of his title. Since his baptism last year, he'd spent much time in prayer and realized that he couldn't marry just **any** woman. No matter how pretty she was.

But, things were different with Vaia. She was intelligent and god-fearing and definitely had a mind of her own. Vaia was the definition of a leader. She brought joy to his heart and made it skip beats. If he wasn't careful, he'd have to put his doctor on speed dial. Even his children loved sharing their day with her.

He knew inviting her to Tuscany was a long shot; given that his mother did not favor their relationship. But he had to ensure that Vaia could handle the pressure of being with him. He often wondered if she knew who he really was.

He wanted to see Vaia again, for her to experience **his** Italy.

Kalevi faced a lot of scrutiny because of his status, but he was determined to pursue this journey with Vaia.

After what seemed like an eternity, she gives him an answer, "Yes, I will come."

"Music to my ears. "How soon can you be here?"

"Whenever you decide."

"I will buy your ticket right away," he volunteers.

"You don't have to do that, I can afford it," Vaia counters.

"I invited you and it is my pleasure. I am honored to have you as my special guest. The children will be ecstatic to see you again. Kaveri is especially excited for you to meet the other *pretty ladies* aka her friends."

"Can I ask you a question?"

Panic began to rise in Kalevi's mind. "G-go ahead," he stutters.

"Are you sure we're not moving too fast?"

"What?"

"This relationship," Vaia answers. "Do you think we're moving too fast?"

"We both know what we want and are on the same page," Kalevi states. "No fast movement, just perfect unison. I love you, Vaia."

She hadn't expected to hear those words and clicked off the call in fear.

19

"Wherefore receive ye one another, as Christ also received us to the glory of God." Romans 15:7

Vaia didn't take long to respond to Kalevi's request. She knew that he wasn't a man who played games and felt comfortable accepting his invitation. Her flight took place two days after he said those three words; **I love you**. Of course she'd apologized for hastily hanging up the call. She still wasn't sure that she'd made the right decision to visit Italy, but trusted that she heard correctly from God.

Kalevi greeted her with a hug. "Welcome back to Italy, *mio amore*. I'll take your bags. How was your flight?"

Vaia allowed him to embrace her. "Slight turbulence. Otherwise, I slept for most of it."

"You are beautiful, wow," he compliments.

"You always say that," she giggles.

"I speak the truth."

"How far are we from my hotel?"

"You'll be staying in the guest house on my estate."

"You have an estate? What do you do for a living?"

"I have somewhere to show you."

"Are we ever going to discuss your job and what exactly you do for the city?" Vaia asks.

"We'll speak about that later. I assure you, you'll understand once as you see my home."

Oh no. I hope this is not a trick...

"Come on," he motions. "I'll take you to see my sister first. She isn't a fan of phone conversations; *too impersonal* she says."

"Where is she?"

"Her job isn't too far from the park where we met."

Out in the distance, Vaia notices a man taking a picture of them entering the vehicle.

"I wonder what that is about," she says aloud.

"What?"

"I just saw someone taking a picture of us."

Kalevi looks at her. "Are you sure?"

"Maybe I'm seeing things," Vaia chuckles. "I mean who'd take a picture of us anyway?"

73 Becoming a Royal Princess

Vaia stares up at the sign, *Gelateria Veneta Lucca.* "I remember this place."

"Oh yeah?"

"I came here the last time I was in Lucca and met a lovely worker."

They walk into the shop.

"*Buon pomeriggio fratello.* I see you've brought a friend," the cashier greets. "Wait a minute, I know this woman. Were you here in May?"

Vaia looks at Kalevi. "This is your sister?"

"*Si signorina,* I am his sister," the woman giggles. "Small world."

Kalevi stares puzzled, his eyes darting between the women. "You two have met?"

"*Si,*" both women reply.

"Brother, no need to introduce us, I like her already."

"This is great news, Arricia," Kalevi exclaims. "She'll be staying on the estate. You should come spend a few days."

"I'll come by soon, I promise," Arricia agrees, taking out gelato for them. "Vaia, do you want the same flavors?"

"Yes, thank you." She looks at Kalevi. "I can't believe she's your sister."

"Unfortunately," Kalevi chuckles.

"Oh whatever brother, you know you love me," Arricia retorts. "I'll see you soon. Enjoy the gelato."

"*Grazie.*" He turns to Vaia. "Let's go."

Something's definitely off. I can't get that cameraman out of my mind. I know those lens were pointed towards us.

"Vaia? Vaia, did you hear me?" Kalevi asks as they walked towards the car.

"Sorry," she replies. "I zoned out."

"You seem to have a lot on your mind. Don't worry; you'll rest when you get to the estate."

Does he work on this estate? What is going on? Why is he so secretive? I don't like this.

20

"If the world hate you, ye know that it hated me before it hated you." John 15:18

Palazzo di Náousa

When the car engine shuts off, Vaia's eyes widen. She began to scan the immense property. There were ancient columns and statues everywhere. Vaia remembered seeing an estate like this in one of her history books. Out in the distance she noted a long walkway leading to a garden filled with a plethora of flowers. This was no regular place.

"Welcome to my humble abode, *Palazzo di Náousa*," Kalevi says, opening the car door.

Vaia's mouth opens in utter astonishment. "You live in a palace? I thought you worked for the city?"

"I do," Kalevi replies.

"Miss Bisenzo, welcome. May I take your bags?" a man dressed in a suit, requests.

Vaia looks at Kalevi. "What's going on?"

"This is Jarvis, Head of Security. You can trust him with your life."

"I'll stick with Jesus, thanks. Why didn't you tell me about all of this, Kalevi?"

"I don't understand."

"You told me that you worked for the city. Yet, I'm standing on palace grounds."

"I do work for the city and I live in a palace because of it," Kalevi counters.

"Why are you acting like this isn't a big deal?" Vaia begins to fan herself. "I need to sit down. I mean who lives in a palace?"

"There are some people I'd like to introduce you to."

"Do I curtsy?" she scoffs. "How do I greet these people? What predicament did I get myself into? I did not sign up for this."

"It's going to be alright, Vaia," Kalevi comforts.

A palace? Wait... is he some kind of royalty or does he work for them? Who is Kalevi?

Moments later, a woman with a regal aura walks to the palace entrance.

"Mother," Kalevi introduces, "meet Miss Vaia Bisenzo. Vaia, this is my mother, Dowager Crown Princess Kavala of Lucca;

Dowager Princess for short. Don't *ever* leave out the Dowager; she views the emphasis as a sign of respect."

Vaia curtsies. "Your Highness."

Kavala waves her off. "All of that isn't necessary Miss Bisenzo. Welcome to our home. Dinner will be served shortly. The maid will escort you to the guest house and you can get changed."

"What's wrong with what I'm wearing?"

"This *look* may work in your country, but here in Lucca we have a standard dress code," Kavala notes with condescension. "You may leave my presence."

"My apologies," Kalevi says, when his mother leaves. "She can be a tad bit dramatic."

"I want to go home," Vaia snaps. "You **lied** to me."

"How did I lie?"

"You said that you worked for the city. If your mother is a Dowager Crown Princess then that makes you a—"

"Crown Prince," he nods.

"You're royalty? As in real life royalty?"

"I thought you said you were royalty, daughter of the Most High God?"

"That's different. You know what I meant. This is not what I expected. I don't want to be a part of this lifestyle. I want to live a drama free life. Not be in tabloids and scandals. That's the only thing I know about royals," Vaia laments.

Kalevi takes her hand. "Don't worry about statuses. I'm still me, Kalevi."

"And besides," Vaia adds, "your mom HATES me. Did you see that scowl on her face when she saw me?"

"Mother doesn't hate you. She just doesn't know you."

"Don't make light of the situation. It's bad enough that we don't look alike."

"I'd hope not; that would be awkward," Kalevi chuckles.

"I'm serious, Kalevi. Our skin tones aren't the same."

"When did that become a challenge for you?"

"The moment I saw the look on your mother's face. You're **royalty**, Kalevi. Your society isn't going to accept a woman who looks like me."

"Do you trust me?" he asks.

"I want to go home," Vaia counters.

As if on cue, Kaveri runs down the hallway and greets Vaia with a big hug. "*SIGNORINAAAAAAAA*. Welcome to our home. This is where *pretty ladies* live."

"Hi pretty lady," Vaia smiles, ignoring the earlier tiff with Kalevi. "How are you?"

"I missed you." She pulls Vaia towards the stairs. "Come on, let's go. I want to show you my room."

Kalevi motions for her to go with Kaveri. "After you show *signorina* your room, please escort her to the guest house so that she can get ready for dinner."

"I'm on it, papa. Let's goooo *signorina*."

"But ye are a chosen generation, a royal priesthood, an holy nation, a peculiar people; that ye should shew forth the praises of him who hath called you out of darkness into his marvellous light..." 1 Peter 2:9

Vaia observes the house in bewilderment. **"This** is the guest house?"

"Yes," Kaveri giggles.

"It looks like an entire apartment building."

"Come on. I want to show you the best part of the palace." Kaveri takes Vaia to the courtyard. "This is where the *pretty ladies* have tea. We have a play date every week and we get to dress up in pretty colors and wear hats. Are you going to join us next week?"

Kalevi walks up behind them and clears his throat. "Kaveri, can I have a moment with *signorina*, alone?"

"Sure papa. I'm going to get dressed for dinner." Kaveri skips off into the distance.

81 Becoming a Royal Princess

It took a few minutes for Vaia to gather her thoughts. "Why didn't you tell me who you were?"

"Would it have made a difference?"

"Uh, yeah. You're **The** Crown Prince of Lucca."

"Why is that so important? I'm still me," Kalevi replies gently. "My status doesn't change anything between us."

"You're acting like it isn't a big deal, but it is. This isn't some fairytale where you *live happily ever after with the prince.*"

"It's not about fairytales. God has blessed me with a platform where I can help people. Isn't that what HE did with Joseph and David and other royals in the Bible? Are you saying that modern day Christians can't have status as well?"

"I'm saying this is too much. You're in charge of an entire monarchy."

"What is the point, *mio amore?*"

"It's already hard being with a **regular** man," Vaia laments, "but you're not regular, so I can't even imagine the pressure of such a relationship."

"And neither are you a regular woman," he replies, gazing into her eyes. "You're God's daughter, Vaia; that's much more important than any earthly title. Why don't you believe it? You've been saying it ever since we met."

"I want to go home," Vaia mumbles.

"I won't force you to stay if you don't want to. But, I want you to stay. And my family does as well," Kalevi counters.

"Your mom doesn't," Vaia snaps.

He takes her hands. "It's just us. Don't include anyone else."

"But why didn't you tell me?" she cries.

Kalevi wipes the tears from her eyes. "I needed to know that you wouldn't be interested in me for my status. Your reaction right now proves to me that I chose well."

"You make it seem so easy."

"Relationships aren't meant to be easy, but we'll get through this together."

22

"Many are the afflictions of the righteous: but the Lord delivereth him out of them all." Psalm 34:19

8PM

"You're early," Kavala chortles. "I'm impressed."

"I don't understand, madam." Vaia motions towards a seat.

"Your **kind**— isn't usually early."

"M-my ***kind***?" Vaia scoffs. "Am I a dog? Where is Kalevi?"

"With his children. Come here," the princess beckons.

"With all due respect madam, please do not speak to me like that."

"You are in MY palace. I will address you however I want."

"I'm still a human being," Vaia retorts calmly.

"The NERVE of this foreigner. I called you, so come," Kavala demands.

Vaia reluctantly walks to the head of the table where Kavala sat.

"Look here you little *RAGAZZA NERA*," Kavala howls, "I'm trying to maintain my composure, but I do not like you. You have **gold digging** social climber written **all over your face**. Stay away from my son. End this charade of an affair you have with him. He's NOT going to marry you. A woman of your kind will **never** inherit anything from this palace. I know you're after his money. I don't want you to **taint** our lineage."

Vaia puts on a facade. "It's sad that in this day and age something like skin complexion and wealth or lack thereof still bothers people. What happened to love, unconditional love? The Bible teaches that we're all the same in God's eyes."

Kavala laughs hysterically. "Bible? I don't believe in that drivel. That's what some people use to help them deal with their low class pathetic status in life. *Oh, we're children of God, we're royalty...*" she laughs snootily. "It's only a matter of time before my son comes to his senses about religion. Mark my words. But you, you will NEVER be part of this family."

"I will pray for you," Vaia responds peacefully. "God loves you. Your hatred isn't towards me. There's a deeper issue. I pray that you deal with it before it's too late."

"HOW DARE YOU SPEAK TO ME LIKE THAT!"

"I haven't raised my voice, madam. But, I am an adult and I want to be addressed as such. I'm not a dog. I'm not a child. I am a grown woman."

Kalevi enters the dining room, oblivious to the heated argument his mother had with Vaia. "I see you two are getting along; sitting next to one another. That's a good sign."

Milos gives Vaia a kiss on her cheek. "Hi *signorina*. You look pretty."

Kavala stands up in haste and marches up to Kalevi. "I want THAT WOMAN OUT OF THIS PALACE THIS INSTANT."

"**That woman** you're referring to is *mio amore* and she will be staying," Kalevi defends.

"Look at what's happening," Kavala huffs. "She's already turning you against me. Sivōrï would've never spoken to me like THAT WOMAN just did. She's UNCOUTH and isn't welcomed here. GET HER OUT."

Kaveri taps her grandmother. "*Nonna*, why are you screaming? You said that ladies don't raise their voice."

"Kaveri, stay out of this," Kavala snaps.

"Mother, you're making a scene," Kalevi says, while comforting his tearful daughter.

"Am I?" she scoffs. "Well no more. I'm leaving. You all can eat dinner with this *RAGAZZA NERA*. I can't have my environment tainted with her filthy existence." She storms out of the dining room.

Vaia begins to cry in humiliation.

"And we know that all things work together for good to them that love God, to them who are the called according to his purpose." Romans 8:28

Kalevi tried his best to pacify the tension. "Children, please excuse me while I talk to *signorina*."

"Okay papa." Milos grabs his sister's hand. "Let's go in the kitchen and eat. Adults are speaking."

"Are you happy?" Vaia blurts, after the children exit.

"What are you talking about?"

In muted sobs Vaia says, "I told you that your mother hates me. I did not sign up for this. I've already experienced being around people who don't like me. I can't marry into a family where my husband's mother hates me."

"You're marrying me, Vaia, not my mother," Kalevi says.

"She's your **mother**, Kalevi. I can't compete with her."

"It's not a competition."

"You don't get it. Men never get it."

"Why are you fighting me?" he inquires.

"How would you feel if Kaveri entered a relationship with a man whose mother hated her?"

"My daughter is strong and she would have to trust the man's love for her. She'd hold on to the fact that God united them. They would be able to face any obstacle once as it's God ordained."

"You can't preach your way out of this. This is real life," Vaia answers.

"Exactly. Real life. Real issues. Real solutions."

"I did not sign up for any of this," she repeats.

"There's no perfect relationship or situation. Love takes work," Kalevi retorts.

"We're not married. I don't have to go through this to be with you."

"Then why are you here?" Kalevi asks. "You thought everything would be like a warm summer breeze? If you can't handle this now, what makes you think you'd be able to handle the trials and tribulations that come in marriage?"

"Don't speak to me like that," Vaia scoffs.

"I haven't raised my voice. Nor did I call you out of your name. Thing is, I love you Vaia, but I won't force you into something that you don't want. I'm a gentleman. It's your decision if you want to stay or go."

"So that's it, huh?" Vaia shrugs. "You're just saying **whatever**. You don't care about my feelings?"

"I'm saying…" He looks into her eyes. "I'm *not* him. I'm not your ex. Stop projecting your fear from the past onto me. I love you. I'm not in this to waste your time."

Tears begin to fill Vaia's eyes. "How could you bring that up?"

"I can see that you're still hurting. Allow God to deal with your hurt fully, but I'm not going anywhere. I love you. And that's a fact."

*That's what you all say until a **better** opportunity comes along. Sigh! Why am I here?*

24

"The Lord is not slack concerning his promise, as some men count slackness; but is longsuffering to us-ward, not willing that any should perish, but that all should come to repentance." 2 Peter 3:9

An hour later, Jarvis opens the front door. In bursts a cheerful princess.

"I'm back."

"Princess Arricia, can I take your bags?"

"Jarvis, you know I hate you calling me that. It's Arricia. I can handle my bags."

"Very well, miss," he nods. "There is dinner in the kitchen when you are ready."

"Thanks. Where's Kalevi?"

"Here," Kalevi responds, entering the foyer to greet his sister.

"Where's Vaia?"

"She's in the guest house packing her bags," Kalevi informs.

"What did you do?" his sister scoffs.

"I didn't do anything, but she's not speaking to me."

"Your guest comes and she's leaving already? Sheesh brother. I'll go speak to her."

Vaia hears a knock on the guest house door.

"Who is it?" Vaia replies, through sniffles.

"Arricia."

"Come in," Vaia motions. "I'm almost done packing."

Arricia plops down on the bed. "Where are you off to?"

"I'm going home," Vaia retorts, tossing her clothes in the suitcase.

"Why? You just got here."

"I don't want to speak about it."

"Come on girl, it's me. Tell me what's wrong."

Vaia stops packing and looks at Arricia. "Your mother hates me. She has said it in many ways that she doesn't want me to be part of this family. My skin complexion and low status are factors in her hatred."

Arricia laughs. "Oh that's all? Mom's a trip. I love her, but that was one of the reasons I moved out of the palace. Of course I'm viewed as the **rebel daughter of the Crown**..."

"What do you mean?"

Arricia gestures for Vaia to sit. "Before papa died he became a Christian and made **a lot** of changes that didn't please mother. Mainly donating money to missionaries and volunteering at soup kitchens. He also paid for homes for the destitute, widowers and orphans alike. Mother accused him of trying to get *sainthood* before he died. Brother and I were baptized last year and this infuriated her more. But, we're her children so she tolerates us, I guess."

"Your dad sounds like a generous man."

"I remember one day he looked at us and said, *'what's the point of having wealth if I don't share with the less fortunate?'* And that made mother angrier. When I told her that I wanted to experience life outside of being a princess and got myself an apartment and a job in the gelateria, she didn't speak to me for months. Eventually, when she realized that I was serious about my decision she came around. At the gelateria I get to meet many people and share my faith with them. No one cares that I am a princess and I like that."

"That's amazing. But, you're her daughter," Vaia says. "I'm not her daughter and I do not look like anyone in this palace."

"Do you have a face? A body? What do you mean you don't *look like* us? Human? You certainly don't resemble a feline. I know it's a lot, but such is life. Christians are persecuted all over the world on a daily basis and here you are crying because someone doesn't like your skin complexion. Get over it. If we live life based on past hurt and pain, we'll never move on as a people. Some people are stagnant because they live in the past. If we say we forgive, then we need to operate in that. God created us all humans, don't allow society to give you your identity. You're not just a box to check on some form or application, you're

God's daughter… God gives you your identity, not man," Arricia states without remorse. "You and my brother are suited. From what he's said, you fit his purpose perfectly. So who else should marry him, but you?"

"You make it sound easy," Vaia sighs, "but it isn't."

"Vaia, *whose report do you believe?* Are you a Child of God or not? Are you royalty or not? I may be a princess on earth, but if I would've died without knowing Jesus, that title couldn't keep me out of hell. Stay. Please."

"I'll think about it."

"No you won't. You're staying," Arricia says, taking clothes out of Vaia's bag, for emphasis. "I'll stay here with you for a few days. We'll handle it together. I want you to be happy. Smile more. You're a beautiful woman. That's why my brother fell in love."

Things would be so much easier if Kalevi's mother liked me.

25

"For the Lord God is a sun and shield: the Lord will give grace and glory: no good thing will he withhold from them that walk uprightly." Psalm 84:11

*Is this really how my life is going to end? I love Kalevi, I do. I don't care if he's a prince. But, why does my love story have to **always** be filled with drama? I could never meet a man and everything just clicks? How could I marry a man whose mother hates me?*

Vaia stands up from the garden bench where she sat after her conversation with Arricia and began pacing the palace grounds.

"God, what is going on with my life? I am a teacher. I'm not a princess. Or any form of royalty for that matter. Yeah, I know that you're the King of Kings and I am royalty in the Kingdom of Heaven, but here on earth... I'm just Vaia Bisenzo. Why me? I'm not special or anything compared to all these beautiful Italian women." She pauses as tears of inadequacy overwhelmed her. "I remember reading the story of Esther, but I'm not her. She didn't seem to have any qualms about her identity. As a matter of fact to me, she was as confident as they came. I know that You confirmed that Kalevi is my husband. You knew that he is a Crown Prince and still You chose **me** to be his wife. Why me? I know this isn't a prayer, but—"

Vaia stopped for a moment as she observed the night sky. She watched as the stars twinkled in the heavens.

"God, You sure know how to create beauty," Vaia chuckles. "I just hope that one day I can feel as beautiful as those stars dancing in the sky. I know that I'm a hot mess right now Jesus, but please help me to see what You see in me. Help me to know why You chose me..."

"There you are, *mio amore*," Kalevi exhales. "I've been looking everywhere for you."

"Here I am," Vaia shrugs.

"You've been crying?" he notes, wiping her tear stained face with a handkerchief from his pocket. "What's wrong?"

"N-nothing. I'm fine now."

"You know that you can talk to me, right?"

Vaia nods.

"Please tell me what's wrong."

"It's just something that I have to deal with on my own," she whispers.

"I'm sorry about earlier. I know that this isn't easy for you. I'm trying to help, but I don't seem to be doing a good job."

"There's nothing for you to do, Kalevi. You can't help it if your mother hates me," Vaia replies, turning her back to him.

Kalevi twirls her around, standing close to her face. "Stop saying that. She doesn't hate you," he counters.

Vaia inhales his scent, stepping back so that she'd be able to think clearer. "Yes. She. Does."

"We're going to get through this. I have to be honest with you, this one's tough. Only God can help me navigate through this situation. She's my mother, you know?"

"I know," Vaia nods. "What can you do?" she chuckles.

"Come on. I have something I want to show you."

"Where are we going?"

"Come on," Kalevi says, gently taking her hand.

26

"And he said unto me, my grace is sufficient for thee: for my strength is made perfect in weakness..." 2 Corinthians 12:9

"Where are we?" Vaia asks, taking in the majestic room. A scene from one of the stories she'd read, came to life.

"This is *la sala dei ritratti reali*, the royal portrait room," Kalevi announces.

"Oh wow. It's beautiful in here." Vaia begins to walk around. "Look at all this history; hundreds of years' worth of portraits." She stops in front of a large painting. "Is that him? Is that your father?"

"Yes," Kalevi smiles. "This is the last painting of His Royal Highness Vasilios Náousa, The Crown Prince of Lucca."

Vaia begins to blush.

Kalevi raises his eyebrows. "Why are you blushing?"

"That's how you're going to look, in the future?"

Kalevi laughs. "Beautiful family, aren't we?"

"I'd say so," Vaia winks.

"You don't have to worry about our future children's looks."

"Who's thinking about children, Mr. Náousa?"

"You'd make a beautiful mother."

Vaia's countenance changes when they stop in front of Kalevi's family portrait.

So that's his wife? Wow. She's beautiful. I have no words.

"And lastly, this is a portrait of my family. This was taken a week before Sivõrï's death." He sighs.

Vaia takes his hand. "We don't have to talk about it. It's okay."

"This picture is always tough for me to see. Do you know she had to beg me to be in it? I told her, *'we have time for photos, let's wait until I come back from my trip.'* But no, she insisted. She said, *'we're not in control of tomorrow, let's do it now.'* Although I'm smiling in the portrait, I was so upset with her. How dare she make demands from the **Crown Prince**? My father had recently passed and I was a mess. I took out my anger on her. It wasn't fair. Who knew that a week later, I'd be burying her too?" He wipes tears from his eyes.

"I'm sorry," Vaia whispers.

"It was at that point I befriended a man I'd considered my father's Pastor. His name is Amerigio Canzoniere. He's from Starr Islands. And he shared the gospel with the family."

"God definitely knows how to get our attention, I can tell you that."

Kalevi nods in agreement.

"Amerigio's been a tremendous help in my life since then. I hope you could meet him one day. He has a wife, son and daughter."

"Why don't you tell me more about Sivõrï, the woman who gave birth to those two children I adore so much?"

"Are you sure? I know it's not easy hearing about her..."

"I'm sure," Vaia replies.

"Where do I begin?" Kalevi exhales.

"I'm going to say good night to Arricia," Vaia states, as they exited the room.

"*Buonanotte amore mio. Sogni d'oro,*" Kalevi whispers in Italian. "Good night my love. Sweet dreams," he repeats in English, kissing her hand.

Vaia knocks on Arricia's door, but overhears a conversation in progress. She pauses at the entrance...

"I can't believe that he took her to the portrait room," Kavala spews. "The last thing I need is for her to think that her likeness will ever end up on those walls."

Arricia pauses her typing. "Did you say something, mother? I'm texting a friend in Sicily."

"What friend? Are you **finally** ready to marry?"

Arricia blushes. "I don't know if we've arrived at that stage in our relationship."

"Please tell me that he is our kind," Kavala scoffs.

"Whatever do you mean?"

"Take your brother for instance and his choice of a potential mate," she whispers.

"What's wrong with Vaia?"

"She's you know... you know..."

"...human?" Arricia finishes. "Is that the word you're looking for?"

"Don't be sass," Kavala hisses.

"I'm lost," Arricia shrugs. "What are you talking about?"

"Oh FINE, I'll say it. She's BLACK. That girl is BLACK."

"Really?" Arricia gasps. "I had no clue. I thought your issue was with her being a foreigner. Mother, you are a sad woman. No one cares about that. When I see Vaia, I see the woman my brother loves. That's all. Whatever prejudice that you have in your heart, you need to deal with it."

"Unreal. Unreal," Kavala huffs. "No one cares about how this looks for the monarchy."

"The monarchy?" Arricia laments. "This is your son's life. You should care more about his happiness than what others think. Everyone loves Vaia. Milos and Kaveri talk about her non-stop. And I'm sure father would've loved her as well."

"Of course you'd bring him up. **Saint Vasilios Náousa, The Crown Prince of Lucca**," she mocks.

"Don't mock father. He was a good man. I am happy that he made the changes he did before his death."

"I'm done with this conversation. If no one in this palace will listen to me, I'll call someone who will."

When she opens the door, Kavala bumps into Vaia. She was standing with tears in her eyes. Obviously she'd overheard their conversation. "HMPH! Now she's eavesdropping. Excuse me, **peasant**!" she barks, pushing past Vaia.

Arricia rushes to hug Vaia.

"I can't do this anymore," Vaia sobs mutely.

"Come in. Let's talk," Arricia replies.

27

"For I the Lord thy God will hold thy right hand, saying unto thee, fear not; I will help thee." Isaiah 41:13

The next morning Vaia woke up to a knock on her door. She hadn't gotten any sleep the previous night, but felt at ease knowing she had an ally in the palace besides Kalevi and his children.

"Who is it?" Vaia calls out.

"It's me, Arricia."

Vaia puts on her robe and walks towards the door. She opened it slowly, so that her morning breath didn't offend Arricia.

Arricia walked towards the vanity seat. "I know that you haven't gotten ready for the morning, but I thought it best to tell you the news in person."

"Tell me what?" Vaia asks, thankful that the woman sat a few feet away.

"I have to leave. An emergency has come up in the shop that I must tend to. My phone's been ringing non-stop."

Vaia's eyes widen. "But, you said that you'll stay to help me. I can't do this on my own. If you're going, so am I. I will call my travel agent now to make arrangements. I'm not ready to face your mother again."

"God is your help."

"I know, but—"

"No buts. Just trust HIM. Everything will work out the way it is supposed to. May I offer you a word of advice?"

Vaia motions for Arricia to finish her thought.

"Whatever happens, you need to remain calm. I don't really know you, but you seem to panic easily."

Wow, she read me like a book.

"It's something that I'm working on," Vaia replies.

"All I know is that when it comes to our Christian walk, we go through the same cycle until we pass the test. Until we learn whatever lesson God is trying to teach us. This is one test that we can't fake our way through."

Vaia nods in acceptance.

"Now that we've gotten that out of the way, Kalevi gave me a message for you. *'Tell Vaia that I'd like to spend some time with her today. And if we can leave promptly at 7:30, it'd be much appreciated.'*"

"Why didn't he text me?" Vaia asks.

"I'm not getting involved. I delivered the message." Arricia looks at her phone. "You have forty minutes to get ready."

"Do you know where he's taking me?"

Arricia shakes her head.

"Great. Now I need to find something worthy of a *prince*."

"Stop that," Arricia scoffs. "Whatever you wear will be suitable. You are royalty. Never forget that."

Vaia sighs, feeling inadequate among the **real royals**.

"See you later," Arricia says, blowing air kisses.

As soon as she closes the door, Vaia scrambles to the bathroom to get ready. She hoped that Kalevi at least gave her time to eat breakfast.

"Did you sleep well?" Kalevi asks, kissing Vaia's cheek. "I'm sorry for what happened last night. I know that this is new for you and I need to be more understanding."

Vaia smiles weakly and looks around. "Where are Milos and Kaveri? Will they be joining us?"

"No. They've gone on an adventure with mother."

"Oh," Vaia exhales, relieved that she didn't have to face the woman who hated her. "So, where are we going?"

"I thought I'd show you around my Italy. We're going to the orphanage, so you can meet some of the children, followed by a true Tuscan tour and then we're going to a restaurant opening. Is that okay with you?" Kalevi asks.

Vaia looks down cringingly at her ensemble.

"What's the matter?" Kalevi asks.

"Can I change? I don't think my outfit is suitable for a restaurant opening," Vaia reveals.

"You look beautiful. I just want you to be comfortable. Don't try to change to fit in. You're *mio amore* and I love you."

"Are you sure?"

Kalevi kisses her hand. "One hundred percent," he winks.

"Why are those people outside of the orphanage?" Vaia squeals, an hour later.

"It's just the paparazzi. Ignore them," Kalevi comforts.

"Prince Kalevi. Prince Kalevi. Who is she? Is she the future Crown Princess? Did you propose?" The paparazzi bombarded them with questions as they walked toward the orphanage entrance.

Once inside, Vaia exhales. "Is it always like this? What gives them the right to invade your privacy?"

"As a public figure, there's only so much privacy that one can have," Kalevi counters.

Vaia yanks her hand away from Kalevi's and looks him in the eye. "I value my privacy to the highest level. I don't know if I can do this. I understand that this is your life, but I'm not sure if I want to go down this path. I feel conned. I didn't know you were a prince when we met and started courting. So, I'm not sure I made the right decision."

"Did you seek the Lord?" Kalevi replies.

"What?"

"Did you ask God if I'm your husband?" he adds.

Vaia nods.

"Then, what's the problem? You asked God and HE answered. I never forced you into a relationship. I didn't lie to you."

"But, you didn't tell me who you really are."

"You still don't understand that being a child of the Most High is a greater status than any earthly one. You are royalty; God's daughter. No one can take that away from you. One day you're going to minister to girls and women alike, reminding them of how special they are. You're going to have such an influence on millions. It's written all over you. And that's one of the qualities that I prayed for in my wife; a woman who is called to serve and impact others; a woman whose compassion transcends status. You have it Vaia. You just need to accept it."

"You sure have a way with words, don't you?"

"It's not about words, *mio amore*, it's about truth; a truth that you'll one day come to accept. I'll keep praying for you."

Am I really that insecure that I need prayer?

106 Becoming a Royal Princess

"Humble yourselves therefore under the mighty hand of God, that he may exalt you in due time: casting all your care upon him; for he careth for you." 1 Peter 5:6-7

"Welcome back, Your Highness. Miss Bisenzo," Jarvis says, later that afternoon. "How was the event, sir?"

"It was wonderful. This beautiful lady here made quite an impression," Kalevi smiles.

"I can see that," Jarvis nods.

"What do you mean?" he replies.

"You are all over the news. Miss Bisenzo is famous," Jarvis chuckles.

"WHAT?" Vaia scoffs. "What news?"

"Come, I'll show you," Jarvis motions.

Vaia paced the kitchen in anger. "This is not happening. This is NOT HAPPENING."

"Calm down, *mio amore*," Kalevi says.

"CALM DOWN? CALM DOWN?" Vaia huffs. "My face is spread all over the news. And look at the caption... ***Crown Prince Kalevi's Chocolate Surprise***. Can you believe this? *Chocolate surprise*? What am I, some kind of dessert? I know that I don't look like you, but really? Is this how the tabloids are? They can just say whatever they want, without any repercussions?"

"None of this matters to me, Vaia."

"Of course it doesn't. YOU'RE not the one who has to deal with racial prejudice. I **AM**. It's my name that's being dragged through the mud here. Not Lucca's beloved **Crown Prince**!"

"Vaia. My beautiful *dulce de leche* Queen," Kalevi chuckles. "I—"

"Did you just laugh? Are you seriously making a joke out of this?"

"Listen to me, woman," Kalevi says firmly. "You're it for me, okay. I love the way you look, everything. What people say doesn't matter. I didn't fall in love with your skin complexion; although I think yours is a perfect design by the Almighty God... I fell in love with you, Vaia Bisenzo, the teacher from Starr Islands. That's it."

Silence filled the room, as his words permeated her soul.

She sighs.

"I know."

"What am I going to do with you?" Vaia asks.

"Kiss me," Kalevi replies.

"Gladly," she giggles.

It was their first kiss and Vaia felt weak in the knees.

"Oooooooo papa and *signorina*," Kaveri squeals. "Kissing like in the fairytales."

"Except this is real life, little sister. Fairytales aren't real," Milos argues.

"Yes, they are," Kaveri counters.

"Nope. I learned that from Ms. Glazier, back in my younger school days."

"What is it that you two are talking about?" Kalevi greets his children at the door.

"I was just telling sister about my younger days," Milos says.

"Is that so?" Kalevi laughs. "So I take it that you're a *big man* now?"

"Uh huh."

"Okay, I guess that I'll just save this present," Kalevi says, holding something behind his back, "for my **young son**."

"Noooo papa. I'm sorry. I'm young, I'm young. Can I please have it?" Milos cries.

"Of course. Take it in the playroom. You and your sister can set it up. *Signorina* and I will join you in a bit."

Milos takes the board game from his father. "Come on Kaveri, let's go."

"Aren't you forgetting something?" Kalevi asks.

"Ooops, sorry *signorina*," the children say in unison, kissing her cheeks.

"Good afternoon, little ones. It's alright. I can see that you're excited to see your father."

The children nod.

"Can we go play now?" Kaveri asks.

"Sure," Kalevi smiles.

Vaia waves to them. "I wonder where they got that excitement from."

"Their mother," Kalevi laughs. Noting the look of sadness on Vaia's face, Kalevi adds, "I know that this is hard for you. Not every woman can marry a widower. I just want you to know how thankful I am for you. Don't ever feel that you have to compete for my attention or that you're a replacement. You're indeed special to me and you came in my life when God wanted you to. I love you, Vaia."

*Is this man for real? He's good looking AND understanding, without me having to spell it out? Of course being labeled a **second wife** or **stepmother** is tough, but I trust God. I just have to keep reminding myself of who I am in Christ. That's what matters the most.*

"But I say unto you, love your enemies, bless them that curse you, do good to them that hate you, and pray for them which despitefully use you, and persecute you..." Matthew 5:44

Seven Days Later

"Is that WRETCH still here?" Kavala yells.

"Watch your language," Kalevi reprimands. "Yes, Vaia is still here. You should get to know her."

"Pish posh. I want her out."

"You sound like a broken record. She's leaving soon, but not for too long. We're planning our life together, so get used to seeing her around."

"I invited the baroness to come stay here indefinitely," Kavala retorts. "You remember Baroness Kinslee don't you? She's a pretty woman of **our** kind. Regal. Everything you need in a wife. Kinslee comes from a reputable lineage. She was Sivōrï's best friend; a perfect replacement for the children's mother."

"No woman can replace their mother," Kalevi answers.

"Isn't that what you're doing with that **whatever** her name is?"

"Her name is Vaia. She isn't here to replace anyone. She's a welcomed addition to the family, my future wife."

Kavala cackles. "I didn't welcome her. I won't sit back and allow that girl to take over this palace."

"She's not a girl. Besides you don't have to *sit back*, you can stand if you want to," Kalevi chuckles. "Either way, Vaia's going to live here eventually."

"OVER MY DEAD BODY!" his mother screams.

"Watch your words, mother. Watch your words. Are you coming with us to the orphanage? Our annual Fall Extravaganza is in a few weeks; we're going over the last minute details."

Kavala wrinkles her nose. "I don't care about any orphans. I don't know why you keep allowing those little BRATS in this palace."

"Don't die a bitter woman. They didn't ask to be in their situation," Kalevi replies.

"Their parents should've made better choices."

Kalevi shakes his head. "See you later. I'll keep praying for you."

"Save your prayers, son."

# 30

"For they intended evil against thee: they imagined a mischievous device, which they are not able to perform."
Psalm 21:11

"Ms. Kinslee," Jarvis greets the baroness, the following day.

"That's **Baroness Kinslee** to you, you pathetic excuse of a man," she scoffs.

"May I take your bags?" he offers, ignoring her insult.

Kinslee creases her nose. "Do you have gloves?"

"Why do I need gloves?"

"I don't want you to actually touch my belongings. Where is the Dowager Princess?"

"Her Royal Highness is in her suite awaiting your arrival," Jarvis informs.

"Well take me to her," Kinslee demands. "She sounded distraught on the phone. What are you people doing to her?"

"Right this way, Baroness Kinslee."

113 Becoming a Royal Princess

When Kinslee enters the room, Kavala claps excitedly. "Baroness, you've arrived. I can breathe again."

"What is the matter, madam?" Kinslee asks, greeting Kavala with air kisses.

"Tell me, when was the last time you spoke to my son? He needs you."

"It's been a while," Kinslee reveals. "What's going on?"

Kavala exhales for emphasis. "Kalevi brought an intruder in our midst and I need you to help me get rid of her."

"What **House** is she from?"

"That's the thing, she isn't of noble blood. She's a teacher from a place called *Lux Point Milano*."

Kinslee signals her displeasure. "Where did Kalevi find her?"

"On his trip with the children," Kavala reveals. "I do not want to speak about her. Let's talk about you. I know you've always loved my son. But you kept your distance when he announced his engagement. His wife is no longer with us and now it's your turn. I've seen many women parade themselves around Kalevi to get his attention, but they weren't a suitable match for him."

Kinslee turns to the window. "The prince doesn't view me that way."

Kavala stands next to Kinslee. "That was when you were being a good friend to Sivōrï, but she's gone and it's time my son's moved on. Preferably with someone he already knows and one who is of noble blood. You fit the description perfectly."

Kinslee's eyes fill with hope. "Do you think he'll have me?"

"He's a man. You're a beautiful woman. Work with what you have. Seduce him. I don't care. Do whatever it takes to get that tart off the premises. Do you understand?"

"I do," Kinslee grins. "Crown Princess has a nice ring to it; Crown Princess Kinslee of Lucca."

"Good girl," Kavala winks. "Now come on. We have a lot to plan with a short timeframe."

31

"And be not conformed to this world: but be ye transformed by the renewing of your mind, that ye may prove what is that good, and acceptable, and perfect, will of God." Romans 12:2

At midday, Kalevi and Vaia enter the palace. His mother stops them.

"Kalevi, there's someone here to see you," Kavala announces.

"Not now. Vaia and I are going to walk in the gardens."

Kinslee steps out from behind a column in the entryway. "Hi Kalevi."

"Good day Baroness Kinslee," Kalevi greets, kissing her hand. "Welcome. To what do I owe the pleasure?"

"I came to visit the children," Kinslee replies.

"That's odd; you haven't been here in months."

"My schedule has finally cleared," the baroness giggles.

"How's your fiancé?" Kalevi asks. "Is he well?"

"We ended our engagement."

"I'm sorry to hear."

Kinslee shrugs. "I have my heart set on a new man."

"Good for you. I wish you nothing but the best. You'll have to invite him to the palace for dinner one day."

"No need to, you already know him," Kinslee blushes.

Vaia clears her throat.

"Oh, I'm sorry," Kalevi apologizes, looking at Vaia. "Baroness Kinslee, this is Vaia, *mio amore*."

"Pleased to meet you," the baroness says, gripping Vaia's hand.

"Likewise," Vaia grimaces. "Kalevi, can we go?"

"Of course," he nods. "Excuse me, mother. Baroness."

"Sure," Kinslee responds, glaring at the couple in disdain.

"I hope you won't be long. We have a guest," Kavala calls out through gritted teeth.

"She's pretty. Why is she here?" Vaia asks when they were out of earshot.

"No need to worry," Kalevi reassures. "It's harmless. She was Sivõrï's friend and she's also close with my mother."

Vaia ignored the hint of jealousy at the mention of his first wife's name.

"She likes you," Vaia states.

"I'm not interested. Now where were we?"

"Be careful with her," Vaia warns.

"The baroness has swarms of men all over her, I'm sure."

"And I'm sure she wishes that you were one of them—"

"Are we going to spend our time talking about the baroness?" Kalevi counters.

I don't know who this baroness is, but I wouldn't put anything past her. She'd better stay away from Kalevi...

"Know ye not that they which run in a race run all, but one receiveth the prize? So run, that ye may obtain."
1 Corinthians 9:24

Later that afternoon, Kinslee made her way up the stairs to Kaveri's playroom.

Part of Kavala's plan was to ensure that the children had a strong bond with the baroness. While Sivōrï was alive, Kinslee had kept her distance. But, since she was no longer in the picture, Kinslee had a chance to become Kalevi's second wife.

Although she despised children, Baroness Kinslee was determined to do whatever it took to win the prince's heart. Her face dropped at the sight of Vaia in the playroom.

Kaveri's face lights up when the baroness enters. "Baroness Kinslee, you're here. Do you know my friend? Isn't she prettyyyyy?"

"Yes, I've met her," Kinslee grumbles. "Your *Nonna's* calling you."

"Okay." Kaveri turns to Vaia. "*Signorina*, I'll be back. Wait right here."

Kinslee closes the door and makes a circle around Vaia. "So you're *THE ONE* huh?"

Vaia rolls her eyes. "Excuse me?"

"I don't know why you're here. Do you **really** think the prince likes you?" Kinslee chuckles. "No, no, no sweetie, you're just a **fill in** until he's ready for marriage again."

"What do you want?" Vaia asks.

"I know your type. You come in; befriend the children and then worm your way into the lonely widower's heart, all just to get the **royal** status."

"Kalevi invited me," Vaia replies. "And I love his children. I'm not 'worming' my way into anything. Save your negativity for someone who cares."

"The Dowager Princess was right about you," Kinslee scoffs. "You really are a **feisty** one. Do you know who you're speaking to?"

"Yes *Miss* Kinslee."

"That's BARONESS to you. What is your title?"

"Vaia Bisenzo, daughter of the Most High God," she announces proudly.

Kinslee laughs. "Do you think I care about your pathetic religious title? I'm being extremely generous with my warning. I don't want you to be embarrassed when Kalevi's eyes open to the truth of what's required as a monarch. Leave this palace and you will be spared global humiliation."

"Are you threatening me?"

"You're very stubborn. One way or the other you're going to leave this palace. If you want to do it the hard way, so be it," she shrugs. "But, I can tell you this... You will NOT be the next Crown Princess of Lucca. **I will**. Why do you think I'm here?"

"Kalevi loves me. Whatever school girl crush you have on him is irrelevant because he's going to marry me and there's nothing you can do about it," Vaia counters.

"We'll see about that—" she huffs.

Kavala knocks on the door. "Baroness, Kaveri is ready for your outing. The limo is waiting outside."

Kinslee holds out her hand to Kaveri. "Come on princess. Let's go."

"Bye *signorina*," Kaveri waves. "See you later."

Vaia looks at them as they walk off.

Kavala grins as she strolls down the hallway. Things were looking in her favor.

Jesus, I need Your help more than ever. Please help me to retain my integrity AND tongue in the midst of this adversity. I don't know what Your plan is in this situation, but please HELP. Amen.

33

"Put on the whole armour of God, that ye may be able to stand against the wiles of the devil." Ephesians 6:11

5PM

"How was the outing with Kaveri?" Kavala enquires.

"She would not stop talking about Vaia."

"Don't worry about it. Kaveri is an impressionable girl, but you'll get through to her. I'm not worried. Once as that **thing** is out of this palace and you're around more often, Kaveri is going to see that *you* are her mother."

"What do you have planned?"

"Go get ready. You leave in an hour." She hands Kinslee a red vial. "You'll need this."

"What is it?"

"Give it to Kalevi to drink. Don't ask any questions."

Kinslee takes the bottle. "Poison?"

"Why would I poison my son? This is a potion that will wash all your worries away. Once as Kalevi drinks it, he'll have no trepidation about you."

"How is that possible?"

"It's a new drug that the palace chemist created. He says that it causes temporary amnesia," Kavala whispers.

"Why would he invent a drug like that?"

"To help people deal with trauma. After I lost my husband, I wanted to forget about all the painful aspects of his death, so I asked him to develop a formula. He tested it on a few subjects and it works."

"That's absurd," Kinslee disparages. "It sounds risky."

"Do you want it or not? The way I see it, if my son forgets about her, you can help him remember what's important, marrying his kind."

"What about his children?"

"Don't worry about the details, my dear. Just make sure that he drinks it," Kavala states, escorting Kinslee out the door.

Kalevi joins Vaia in the guest house.

"You look snazzy in your tuxedo," Vaia compliments. "Where are we off to? How long do I have to get ready?"

"I'm afraid you're not invited," Kalevi apologizes, kissing her cheek.

123 Becoming a Royal Princess

Vaia's face falls flat. "What?"

Kalevi explains the situation.

"What do you mean you're going out with **her**?" Vaia snaps.

"My mother has asked that the baroness represent her at a charity ball. And I am her escort for the evening," Kalevi replies. "I forgot that it was tonight."

"Don't you see what's happening?" Vaia laments. "Do you have to go?"

"Duty calls, *mio amore*."

"I don't like this. Can't you go alone?"

"No."

Vaia huffs in anguish. "I can't believe that you don't see what's going on. Your mother is perfectly capable of attending the ball, why does Kinslee have to go?"

"I don't know. Mother's getting down in age. This isn't the first time she's sent someone in her stead."

Getting down in age... Yeah right. She knows exactly what she's doing.

"Well, then she should contact that person," Vaia retorts.

"I'm afraid that's not how things work."

"You sound really happy to be escorting *Miss Kinslee*."

"I can handle myself," Kalevi responds. "Don't you trust me?"

"You, I trust." She points to the palace. "It's Kinslee that I don't trust."

Kavala knocks on the door. "Kalevi, are you ready? It's getting late."

"I'll be right out, mother."

"I can't believe this. You're **actually** going."

Kalevi kisses her forehead. "I will be back *mio amore*, I promise."

As the limo pulls off, Vaia sighs.

"You may as well pack your bags now," Kavala laughs.

"Madam, what have I done for you to hate me so much?"

"Oh SHUT UP!" Kavala walks back into the palace, smirking.

2AM

Kinslee knocks on Kavala's bedroom door. "Are you up?"

"Come in, come in. How did it go?" Kavala asks. Although she hadn't expected them to spend that long at the event, she was eager to hear what transpired.

"Everything went well, but he did not drink it."

"That potion was our last resort," Kavala grunts.

"Not exactly. I have a plan."

"Do tell," Kavala chuckles.

"Just wait and see, Your Highness."

"Proactive. Now **that** is the marking of a Crown Princess."

The women giggle.

34

"There hath no temptation taken you but such as is common to man: but God is faithful, who will not suffer you to be tempted above that ye are able; but will with the temptation also make a way to escape, that ye may be able to bear it."
1 Corinthians 10:13

When Kalevi enters the kitchen, the next morning, he heads to the oven to cut a slice of *Macadamia Cloud Torte*. For a grown man he sure had a sweet tooth.

He sat down on the stool reading the day's newspaper. His face fell flat as he stared at the headline news: **Has The Crown Prince Found His Princess?** The article had a photo of him and Kinslee dancing at the ball.

What would Vaia think when she sees this?

He didn't notice the baroness watching him from the entrance of the kitchen.

When she entered, he gulped. Though he loved Vaia and knew he wouldn't give in, Kalevi didn't want to give the enemy **any** room to work.

It finally dawned on him that maybe Vaia was right about Kinslee.

Jesus, please help me pass this test.

Baroness Kinslee smiled as she knew that her ensemble caught Kalevi's attention. The clingy dress was enough to drive any man mad with passion. It had a plunging neckline and slits in the right places. She'd do **anything** to get the prince's attention. A smirk crossed her face as she gazed at the headline news, happy she'd hired the paparazzi to take their picture for the front page. Of course she'd never tell Kalevi about this. "*Buongiorno*, Your Highness." Kinslee curtsies. "Can I join you for a slice?"

"That won't be necessary." Kalevi stands. "I was about to leave."

"Oh please Kalevi, it's me. I just want to have a snack with my friend."

"Why are you still here? Don't you have duties back home?"

"This is all part of my duties," Kinslee flirts.

"You've stated that you came to keep my mother company. Why is it that you're always around me?"

The baroness stands next to him and bends down. Kalevi instantly turns his eyes away.

Kinslee laughs. "Why'd you look away? Am I not desirable?"

"I love Vaia."

"That's not what I asked. And I know that you love her. I don't mind sharing for now. She doesn't deserve you. How could you love that commoner?"

"Vaia is royalty," Kalevi replies.

Kinslee takes a bite of the torte. "I see that you got over Sivōrï quickly."

He pushes the plate away, suddenly losing his appetite. "Don't you dare say that! You know how much my wife meant to me."

"I'm sorry Kalevi," Kinslee says, rubbing his hand. Kalevi yanks it away.

"Kinslee, whatever you're trying to do won't work. Instead of trying to seduce another woman's husband, why don't you wait until you're found by **your** husband?"

"You sound weak," Kinslee laughs. "Besides, who says that you're that commoner's husband?"

"Your opinion matters not. I don't need to explain anything to you."

Kinslee throws herself onto Kalevi. "Kiss me, NOW!"

"Kalevi?" Vaia shrieks when she enters the kitchen.

He instantly turns and Kinslee lets go of his neck.

"You can have him for now." Kinslee rolls her eyes as she proceeds to exit the kitchen. "We look good together don't we, Kalevi?" Kinslee chuckles, glancing down at the newspaper.

129 Becoming a Royal Princess

Kalevi runs to Vaia, hoping she hadn't seen the photo. "*Mio amore,* it's not what it looks like."

"Usually when a man says that, it's **exactly** what it looks like."

"I'm telling you the truth," his Italian accent spilled from his lips.

"You've allowed this woman to stay here even after I've voiced my qualms. She obviously has ill motives. Now this? ARE YOU KIDDING ME?"

"She's here to keep my mother company."

"I know you're not that naïve, Kalevi. No, I refuse to believe that you're trying to justify why I walked in to see my future husband with another woman wrapped around his neck. How disrespectful. Do you care about me at all? If you want to cheat, at least have the decency to go somewhere else."

"I didn't cheat on you. Kinslee threw herself at me."

"You obviously entertained her advancements."

"You weren't even here," Kalevi says. "I told her to leave. I tried to leave. She came and met me here."

"Are you hearing yourself? You sound like a teenager."

"You're calling me immature?"

"No, I'm saying— You know what... It doesn't even matter anymore. If you cared about me, she wouldn't have stayed past hello. How would you feel if I brought a male **friend** to stay in my house?"

"Why are we arguing? Will you listen to me?"

"I don't want to hear it," Vaia snaps. "Your actions are **screaming** louder than your words. Don't think that I didn't see that picture either. You DANCED with her?"

Kalevi interlocks their hands, gazing into her eyes. "*Mio amore*, I love you and only you. Do you really think I would jeopardize what we have? It was just an innocent dance; representatives of the Crown."

"I bet it was."

"We have to learn to trust one another in order for this relationship to work."

Vaia stands without saying a word, allowing the tears to fall from her eyes.

Kalevi wipes her tears and kisses her forehead. "I love you Vaia. I don't want anyone else."

"I can't keep doing this," she sobs. "It's too much. It's not supposed to be this hard."

"We'll get through it. Anything that comes our way, we'll get through it together."

"Do you promise?" Vaia asks.

Kalevi embraces her. "I promise."

35

"Have not I commanded thee? Be strong and of a good courage; be not afraid, neither be thou dismayed: for the Lord thy God is with thee whithersoever thou goest." Joshua 1:9

"Are you excited for your tea party tomorrow?" Kalevi asks his daughter.

"Yes papa. The *pretty ladies* are excited."

The chef knocks on the playroom door. "What would you like me to bake for dessert, sir?"

"Chocolate cake with coconut slivers," Milos blurts, jumping on his chair.

"Sit down Milos," Kalevi reprimands.

"Sorry papa," the boy apologizes.

"Where is *Nonna*?" Kaveri cries.

Kalevi comforts his daughter. "Not to worry. *Nonna* will be back before dinner time."

Kinslee had been at the palace for a few days devising her plan with the Dowager Princess.

"When will this brilliant plan of yours go into motion?" Kavala asks over the phone.

"Don't worry, I've got everything under control," Kinslee smirks, applying her lipstick and scanning her face in the mirror.

"You're working a bit too slow for my liking."

"Trust me, I got this."

Kavala clicks her tongue. "Time's ticking. I will see you when I return to the palace."

"Yes madam." Kinslee smiles. One way or the other, Kalevi was going to fall in love with her.

After lunch, the chef brings out the specially requested dessert for the family. "Enjoy," he states, before returning to the kitchen.

Kalevi cuts the cake and hands a slice to everyone at the table.

"*Questa torta ha un sapore così buono. Lo adoro,*" Milos states excitedly.

"*Sì* Milos," Kalevi nods. "It is a good cake." He turns to look at Kaveri.

"Wait for me," Kaveri chimes. "I haven't taken a bite yet."

"Well, hurry," her brother says, in between chewing.

"Here goes." Kaveri takes a bite of the cake. "Hmmm this tastes good." Suddenly she begins to gag.

Kalevi runs to her side. "Kaveri. Kaveri," he cries. "What's wrong?"

Kaveri falls out of her chair, gasping for air.

"Jarvis, call the ambulance," Kalevi calls out.

Kalevi paces the hospital hallway in tears at the thought of losing his daughter. They'd been sitting in the waiting room for two hours.

"*Amore*, everything will be fine," Vaia encourages, holding his hand.

"I've already lost two persons I love," he sobs. "I can't bear the thought of losing another."

Vaia ignores the slight tinge of jealousy, knowing that one of those *loved ones* was Kalevi's first wife.

"Where is she?" Kavala barks, charging into the hospital waiting room. "Where is my granddaughter?"

"We're still waiting on the news," Kinslee replies, while staring at Kalevi and Vaia cuddling.

Kavala greets Kinslee. "Thanks for calling me."

"Of course madam," the baroness answers.

Kavala stares at Vaia and furiously yells, "WHAT IS SHE DOING HERE?"

Kalevi motions for his mother to be quiet. "Can we please keep the focus on Kaveri?" he asks.

Kavala whispers to Kinslee, "I thought you had a plan?"

"My plan has already been put into place," the baroness grins.

"After we leave here, we'll discuss it further," Kavala murmurs.

No one noticed the time on the clock, as time stood still. Finally the doctor came outside.

"Sir, can we speak privately?" Dr. Trasilc requests.

Kalevi sighs and follows the doctor into his office.

When Kalevi returned to the waiting room, his mother worriedly asks, "What did the doctor say?"

"Based on what he said, it appears as though someone deliberately tried to kill Kaveri with *Thalak Seeds*."

Kavala gasps. "But, she's allergic to it. When your father brought it home and she had that reaction all those years ago. It was banned from Italy."

"I know," Kalevi responds, angrily.

36

"Let not your heart be troubled: ye believe in God, believe also in me." John 14:1

Thirty Minutes Later

"*Buonasera signore e signori*, my name is Detective Bruyére. Jarvis has brought me up to speed."

"Welcome Detective," Kalevi says.

"Is there any update?" the detective asks.

"We're currently waiting on the lab results."

Detective Bruyére makes a note in his notepad.

"Looks like the doctor has gotten the results," Kalevi states, as Dr. Trasilc walked towards them.

Vaia holds Kalevi's hand in support. She didn't know what to say in a time like this, but knew that being there for Kalevi would matter a great deal to him.

Detective Bruyére walks towards the nursing station. "Seal off all exits. No one is to come on or leave this floor."

A nurse nods at him.

"If I may interject—"

"Not now Kinslee," Kalevi retorts, trying to keep his anger at bay. He couldn't believe that someone tried to kill his daughter.

"I know who did this," she contends.

Kalevi nods. "Yes, it was the chef. He will be arrested."

"No. No," Kinslee shakes her head in disagreement. "Think about it. Who is the only one among us that would have access to *Thalak Seeds*? You know, seeds only found in **Starr Islands.**"

Kalevi drops Vaia's hand.

Vaia begins to panic. "Are you seriously accusing me?"

"If the spoon mixes," Kinslee scoffs.

Vaia looks at Kalevi. "You can't honestly think that I'd do something like this."

"*Thalak seeds* come from Starr Islands. They don't sell it in Italy," he replies.

Detective Bruyére stares at Vaia. "Ma'am, I'd have to ask you to come with me."

"On what grounds?" Vaia laments.

"Please don't make a scene," Detective Bruyére adds.

137 Becoming a Royal Princess

Vaia begins to cry. "Kalevi, you promised..."

Kavala points at Vaia. "You see what I was saying all along? This girl is NO GOOD. Detective, you need to get her off the premises and out of this country before she tries to kill ANOTHER member of my family."

"Ka—" Vaia tries to call Kalevi, but he ignores her.

"Ma'am, you'll have to come with me," Detective Bruyére says to a tearful Vaia.

The baroness shakes her head. "This is what happens when you intermingle with the poor. They don't know how to conduct themselves and would do ANYTHING to get ahead in life. Is she going to prison?"

"Not now Kinslee," Kalevi retorts. "You're not helping the situation."

"B-but—" Kinslee starts, but stops when she sees the look on Kalevi's face.

Vaia reaches out to Kalevi. "I didn't do it, my love. I promise. You promised me that we'll work out anything that comes our way."

Kalevi yanks his arm away from Vaia's touch. "I TRUSTED you and you repay me by trying to KILL MY CHILD. YOU PUT HER LIFE AT RISK? GET OUT OF THIS HOSPITAL, NOW!"

"That's right. GET OUT!" the Dowager Princess yells.

The detective hauls Vaia away in handcuffs.

37

"But the fruit of the Spirit is love, joy, peace, longsuffering, gentleness, goodness, faith, meekness, temperance: against such there is no law." Galatians 5:22-23

"Vaia. Vaia. Can you tell us about your relationship with the Crown Prince of Lucca? Did you try to kill his daughter? Ms. Bisenzo..."

Vaia runs inside, tired of the constant swarm of paparazzi in front of her house. It surprised her that the prince hadn't pressed any charges, but she did receive a restraining order to cease all contact with the royal family. Her relationship with the prince was over before they built a deep foundation. Who was she kidding to ever think that she could marry a man with Kalevi's status, though she had no prior knowledge of it and loved him in spite of?

Weeks had passed since Vaia left the Italian hospital in utter humiliation. Kalevi ignored every attempt that she made to contact him. Of course this was before she received the letter of restraint. He'd even deleted her from his **Avenami** account and blocked her from every other form of contact they had. It was the worse feeling in the world. It hurt her even more than what transpired with her ex-fiancé, Easton.

Vaia's brother and his wife reached out to her, but speaking to her loved ones added fuel to the pain. However, Veria was not someone who would take the hint. She moved in with Vaia when she returned from Italy. No questions asked. Her mother did not take no for an answer. Even though it annoyed her, deep down inside, Vaia was glad for the company.

"Those people clearly have no lives. Do you want me to call the police?" Veria offers.

"The police told me that as long as no one **actually** steps foot on my property then there's nothing they can do."

"I will go to higher authorities if this persists. Look at the mess you've put yourself in. You never listen to me," her mother mumbles.

"Not now," Vaia exclaims.

"Yes, now! Right now! Look at the public spectacle that you've become. You got yourself involved with those *royals*," she mocks, "and they throw you out at the first chance they get. They didn't even give you a chance to defend yourself. **That's** what you want for your life, global humiliation?"

"What do you want me to do?" Vaia snaps. "It doesn't even matter. I'm glad that they didn't have me thrown in prison."

"You're innocent. You love children and I know you'd never do anything to hurt anyone."

"My innocence isn't going to erase the barrage of paparazzi outside."

"Take a break from relationships. Do you see what happens when you try to enter into *their* world?" Veria replies. "I told you that chocolate and vanilla do **not** mix."

"Please stop," Vaia cries. "Like seriously, please stop."

"You will never be accepted into their society. Stay with your own kind."

"What **kind**? You mean *humans*? We're all humans."

"You look foolish, crying over that prince," Veria counters. "It was all a fantasy. Can't you see? I bet you he's going to marry the baroness. That's how life goes, sweetie. We don't always get what we want. I thought you learned this already. Guess I was wrong."

"I SAID STOP! I have enough to deal with. I don't need this from you. You're supposed to be helping."

"You're yelling at me when I'm the one who has been with you after BOTH of your failed relationships? When I'm the one that helped you pick up the pieces of your broken heart from **your** choices. I can't believe THIS is the thanks I get. Why did I end up with such a FOOLISH daughter?" Veria barks.

"I never asked you to help me. Not once."

"Ungrateful."

"Having this conversation with you will not change anything," Vaia laments. "God knows what will happen. I trust HIM."

"You're joking," Veria laughs. "God didn't put you in this mess. You did."

"If you don't have anything constructive to say, I'm asking you to leave so that I can spend time in prayer and fasting to salvage my pitiful life."

"What an embarrassing position you've put me in as your mother. I'm now a laughing stock in this community."

"Are you seriously making this about yourself?" Vaia shrieks.

"Yes, I am," Veria nods profusely. "Do you know how humiliating it is to be known as the mother of the woman who almost **killed** a princess?"

"Unbelievable," Vaia scoffs. "I can't deal with this right now. I'm going to my room."

"That's all you do, RUN. Why didn't you have all that mouth to defend yourself to that royal family, huh? Instead you came back home to disrespect me, the woman who gave birth to you."

"This is **my house**. What are you talking about?" Vaia rolls her eyes.

"We'll talk about this when I get back. I have errands to run."

You don't need to come back. Why is this happening?

38

"Blessed are they which do hunger and thirst after righteousness: for they shall be filled." Matthew 5:6

One Month Later

"One *Cobalt Tea,* please," Vaia asks the cashier at *Last Drop Tearoom.*

"That will be $1.50."

"I'll take care of that," a man offers.

"It's alri—" Vaia's mouth drops open.

"Yes, it's me," the man greets. "Easton, in the flesh."

The cashier hands Vaia her tea. "Next on line."

Walking over to a table, Vaia sits across from her ex-fiancé.

"You look lovely, Vaia. I missed you."

"Easton, what are you doing here? I thought you moved back home?"

"I think the universe wants us to be together. I've been seeing your face all over the media. I had to come and see you. I know you ended our relationship, but I should've fought for us. Being without you for over a year has had me thinking."

"Thinking about what?" Vaia grimaces. "I'm not interested in whatever you have to say. I'm not the same woman you left last year."

"Doesn't matter," Easton shrugs. "I'm not the same man you broke up with. I want you back. I still love you." He reaches out to touch her hand.

"**Love**?" Vaia laughs. "You never loved me."

"You broke up with me, Vaia. I didn't want things to end."

"You gave me no choice."

"You never gave us a chance," he responds.

"What **us**? I broke up with you and you didn't even hesitate to jump in that taxi and leave."

"That was the past," Easton recounts. "I want us to start over. I've taken a sabbatical from work to salvage our relationship. I'm going to do whatever it takes to show you that I love you and want us to work. I want you to come with me to *Voque*. We can build a house and do all the things we planned before you broke things off."

"There's nothing to salvage. If I thought something was worth fighting for, I would not have ended it. You chose *work* over me. I can't live my life playing second fiddle to your career."

"I'd leave it all behind just to be with you," he counters.

"No need. I'm not interested. Good bye."

"We can work things out."

"Let go of my hand," Vaia snaps. "I have to go."

39

"For God is not the author of confusion..." 1 Corinthians 14:33

Veria's House

"Mrs. Bisenzo, may I come in?" Easton asks, a few hours later.

"What are you doing back in *Lux Point Milano*?"

"I came for Vaia."

"Let me guess, you saw her pictures **everywhere**?"

"Who is this PRINCE that has taken her heart away from me?"

"Young man, you lost her heart on your own," Veria scoffs. "I saw how you treated my daughter. Why are you here?"

"Help me win her back," Easton pleads.

"No."

"I love Vaia. I want to marry her."

"She's not the same woman you left. You don't stand a chance."

146 Becoming a Royal Princess

"That's what she said to me. What does that mean? She looks the same."

"Vaia's a Christian now," Veria replies. "She's not going to associate herself with a man who doesn't share her beliefs. Believe me; I've tried hooking her up."

"Oh that's fine," Easton chuckles. "I go to church on holidays. We can work that out. That's a small matter."

"Not according to her."

"Tell me about this prince. Who is he? How can I get in contact with him? We need to have a man to man talk. I want to look him in the eye and tell him to leave Vaia alone."

"There's nothing to talk about. They haven't communicated in almost two months," Veria reveals.

Easton begins to shiver. "It's starting to get chilly outside. Are you going to invite me in?"

"I guess you didn't get the *'you're not wanted'* hint," Veria remarks.

"I'm a determined man this time around. No Bisenzo woman is going to ignore me."

"Fine. Come in. But only because I know that you love drama and I don't need any more embarrassment in my life." Veria opens the door to let him in.

40

"And no marvel; for Satan himself is transformed into an angel of light. Therefore it is no great thing if his ministers also be transformed as the ministers of righteousness; whose end shall be according to their works." 2 Corinthians 11:14-15

"The baroness would make a wonderful wife. Why have you been ignoring her?" Kavala enquires.

"Why is she still here? Has she no home of her own? She's been here for more than two months. It's not appealing for a woman to just give up her life to be with me."

"I hope this isn't about that stupid Starr Islands woman. She tried to KILL your daughter. Are you forgetting that part?"

"We have no proof of that," Kalevi defends.

"Unbelievable," Kavala shakes her head. "She's not even here and has you wrapped around her finger. I'm beginning to wonder if she did something to you."

"Are you implying some sort of magic?"

Kavala nods. "It's the only logical explanation."

"You're not behaving like my mother. I don't know what has gotten into you, but you need to get the baroness out of this palace because I don't want to marry her."

"Look at you walking around depressed all because of that stupid low class woman. **Grow up**. You're a father for goodness sake. What will your children think of you?"

"Leave my children out of this. Do you have anything else to say? I'm done with this conversation. I need to pray and ask God to help me. I can't continue living like this."

Kavala claps sarcastically. "For once, I actually agree with you. Go pray. I honestly think only your *god* can get you out of your misery."

When Kavala exits the prince's study, Kinslee walks up to her and says, "I think it's time that I go back home. All that we've tried and the prince hasn't even looked at me differently. He's still pining over her."

"If you want to be a Náousa you can't be weak," Kavala snaps. "You have a golden opportunity here and you're squandering it talking to me. My son is vulnerable, you're a woman. **Use it to your advantage**. Now go fix yourself up. You look awful."

Taking Kavala's advice, Kinslee spots Kalevi on the balcony and decides to try again to win his heart.

Kalevi sighs when he sees the baroness walking towards him.

Jesus, please help. I'm not strong enough to deal with anything...

"Mind if I join you?" Kinslee asks, staring at Kalevi.

He turns towards her. "Baroness Kinslee, with all due respect, I don't want to talk."

"Is it about her?" she inquires, touching his arm. When he pulls away she removes her hand. "Wow, this woman has you enchanted. What is it about her?"

"I don't want to talk."

"Come on, aren't we friends? It's not good to keep things bottled up inside. You can talk to me, I won't bite," she chuckles.

"Why are you still here?" Kalevi asks. "I just don't get it. You allegedly came for my mother, but every time I turn around, I see your face."

"Don't you see that we're meant to be? I'm not here by chance. It's kismet."

"I understand that you're heartbroken over your shattered engagement, but please don't use me as your rebound man. You deserve much better."

"You do not understand Kalevi; it's you that I want... It's always been you," Kinslee reveals.

"I'm sorry Kinslee; I've never viewed you as anything but a friend of the family. Please excuse me as this area is too full for me to continue my meditation."

Kinslee stares at the prince walking away from her, noting that there was nothing she could do to win his heart. It was time for her to return home...

41

"Every word of God is pure: he is a shield unto them that put their trust in him." Proverbs 30:5

"What is he doing here?" Vaia asks her mother, a few days later. "I thought that I was the only one over for dinner. But, I see you have company," Vaia scoffs.

"Don't speak about my house guest in that tone," Veria answers.

Vaia pulls her mother into the foyer. "He's staying here?"

"Why not? I have the spare bedroom and he's been quite handy around the house."

"Handy with what? You don't have anything to fix."

"He buys groceries, drives me wherever I want to go—"

"Don't you see what's happening?" Vaia asks.

"Easton's trying. I know that I didn't like him before, but he's changed," Veria smiles.

"HA! Easton changed?"

"Doesn't your Bible speak of people changing?"

"Yes," Vaia nods. "But what change have you observed in him? He's still the same calculating man that I knew."

"How could you say that about him?"

Easton enters the foyer with an oven mitt on his hand. "You ladies alright?"

"Give us a minute," Veria replies.

"Okay, Mrs. Bisenzo," Easton nods, walking back to the kitchen.

"See. Look at that. He came to see how we're doing. He's thoughtful and considerate."

"Then **you** marry him," Vaia states.

"Give him a chance honey, you never know."

"I love Kalevi."

"STOP IT with that man. He dumped you, remember? He kicked you out of his palace. Had you fly thousands of miles to be with him, then almost had you imprisoned. Why didn't he come to see you here? Huh? Some gentleman he is. Now look at you obsessing over him like an idiot."

Vaia walks towards the kitchen. "I'm hungry. I don't want to speak about this anymore. After this meal, I'm going back home."

"What a scrumptious meal, Mrs. Bisenzo," Easton compliments.

"Why don't you call me Veria?"

"I have too much respect for you, madam."

"Whatever suits you," Veria chuckles. "Why don't you two go for a drive while I clean up?"

Easton looks at Vaia. "That sounds good, but it's up to her."

"I'll help you with the dishes, mom. Then I'm going **home**."

"Go for a drive," Veria repeats.

"B-but," Vaia stutters.

Veria gives her daughter a look. "I said GO!"

Easton parks his car by the riverside and turns to Vaia. "Remember when we went to that 3D gallery and you were afraid to step in the elevator because you thought it was full of sharks?"

Vaia laughs out loud. "That's a traumatic memory for me. It's not funny."

"Yet you're laughing." He pauses before stating, "I miss this. I miss us. You're still as beautiful as the day we met. Do you remember that day?"

"How could I forget? You were on your phone and bumped into me, sending my briefcase and all of its contents flying."

"Do you remember what you told me after?"

"Yes. *You'll have to—*"

"*—pay for this,*" Easton finishes.

"I'm not saying we didn't have good times. But I can't compete with your work. That's why I ended our relationship."

"I was stupid then. However, in my defense I did it for us. I was taught that a man provides for his family. As my wife you're my family."

"I'm not your wife," Vaia corrects.

"Not yet. We can change that." He leans in for a kiss.

"Easton, no— I can't."

"Is it him?"

"This isn't about Kalevi. You and I are no longer compatible."

"We've always been compatible," Easton smirks.

"What I mean is... You're not a Christian."

"I can go to church more often," he offers.

"It's not just about going to church, but serving Jesus Christ wholeheartedly."

"I can get to know Jesus. Tell me about him. I'd do anything to be with you."

"That's not how things work."

"Can we at least try? What's the harm in trying?" Easton asks.

42

"Do not be yoked together with unbelievers. For what do righteousness and wickedness have in common? Or what fellowship can light have with darkness?" 2 Corinthians 6:14

"It's been two weeks and I've been seeing a lot of Easton. This is a good sign," Veria states.

"It doesn't mean anything," Vaia replies.

"The man says he wants to do things the right way."

"Staying at a hotel doesn't constitute as doing things the right way. I don't know why he's doing all of this."

"He extended his sabbatical. If that's not effort, I don't know what is. When are you going to say yes to a relationship with him? What more does he have to do to prove his love? He's even gone to church with you every Sunday since he arrived."

"If he accepts Jesus as his savior I would be happy for him, but it shouldn't be for me."

"I don't know what your problem is. You're clocking 31 and still no wedding in the works. What are you waiting for?"

"There's no peace in my heart to be with Easton. As a matter of fact I see **RED FLAGS**!"

"Pray and ask your *god* to change Easton so you can get married."

"God isn't a genie and I will **not** pray against HIS will. I know Easton isn't the one for me."

"You're still on that Italian prince?"

"I don't know who my husband is, but it isn't Mr. Easton Tekir. So can we drop the subject?"

The next day, Easton enters a jewelry store determined to pick a ring for Vaia. Although he knew they weren't at that point, he wanted to be prepared.

"Good day sir," the jeweler greets. "How may I help you?"

"Can I see your engagement rings selection?"

"Do you have a budget?"

Easton pulls out his bank card. "Money's not an issue for me."

The jeweler takes his card. "Please follow me."

"Hi Easton, where are you?" Vaia asks over the phone.

"I'm home."

"Were you going to tell me?"

"I'm coming back to you soon. There was something I had to take care of here," he says, looking at the ring he just purchased.

"Save it," Vaia retorts. "Stay wherever you are. Don't bother to come back."

"What? I-I can't hear you—"

"Easton? What's that noise in the background? Hello? Hello?"

He didn't change at all. What am I thinking? Vaia don't waste anymore of your life on this man. Haven't you learned your lesson?

43

"Watch and pray, that ye enter not into temptation: the spirit is indeed willing, but the flesh is weak." Matthew 26:41

8:30PM

The ringing of the doorbell pierced through the living room. Putting down her book, Vaia heads to the door.

I'm not expecting anyone.

Vaia opens the door to Easton. "I thought—"

He puts a finger to her lips. "Surprise."

Batting off his hand, Vaia stands akimbo. "I thought you were back in *Voque*?"

"I was on the airport when we spoke. I wanted to surprise you. Pack your bags. We're going on a trip."

Vaia tilts her head. "What trip? I have to work."

"I called your supervisor and asked for today off. We'll only be gone for the weekend."

"What is this about?"

Easton enters the house. "Where is the one place that you've always wanted to go?"

"Italy," Vaia mumbles. "I went there already."

"On a private jet?"

Vaia stares at him. "Can you get to the point?"

"I'm taking you on a weekend getaway. We'll be back in time for you to go to work on Monday."

"Since when do you care about my work? Why did my boss give you permission?"

"I'm a convincing man," he chuckles.

More like conniving.

"How'd you know that I'd say yes?"

"It's Italy, Vaia. I know you love Italy. You told me that you didn't get a chance to explore it fully during your cruise. So I want to change that."

"You mean the cruise we were supposed to go on together?" Vaia sighs, ignoring the pain from the hurt of their breakup.

"We're both to blame for that, but no worries. This will be a grand weekend."

"No surprises." She points to his pocket. "You're not going to propose or anything, right?"

"We haven't reached that stage yet. We're starting over."

"I can't stay in a room with you. It's not going to be like before."

"I know, I know." He takes her hands. "I respect your beliefs. That's why I rented **two** different suites for us to stay in. So pack your bags, we're going to Italy."

Am I doing the right thing? Oh well, what harm could be done? He knows where I stand. He did say we'd be in different suites, so nothing to it…

Sicily, Italy

"We're here," Easton announces when the jet landed.

"It's beautiful," Vaia squeals. "I didn't come off the ship when it docked here the last time."

"We're spending our first time in Italy together."

Vaia gives him an unpleasant look.

"What's wrong?" he asks.

"This was the port where Kalevi and I spoke before—" she reminisces.

"I didn't bring you here to speak about another man," Easton snaps.

Vaia looks around. "Where's our hotel?"

He points to the beautiful mansion they stood in front of. "We'll be staying in this villa. I rented it for us."

"Here? I don't want to stay anywhere with you alone."

"We won't be alone. As you can see, the villa is huge. There will be chefs, a butler, driver... We won't be alone."

"Oh great," she grumbles. "We're playing house."

"Benvenuto Sig. E Sig.ra Tekir," the villa owner greets in Italian.

"Non sono sua moglie," Vaia responds, happy she'd been studying the language.

"I'm sorry madam," the owner apologizes. "I thought you were married. This is a honeymoon villa."

"A WHAT?" She shoots Easton a piercing glance. "Eas—"

"Shh, shhh," he says, placing his finger on her lips. "It's fine. It's the largest place I could find on such short notice, where we can get our own suites."

"May I take your bags to your rooms?" a bellhop requests.

Easton nods. "You can place her bags upstairs. I will be downstairs. I'm her protector."

The bellhop smiles. *"Certo signore."* He places their bags on a cart.

Vaia pulls Easton to the villa entrance and voices her disapproval of the situation. "A honeymoon villa, really? We're not having sex or anything remotely close to it, do you understand?"

Easton holds up his hands. "Hands off policy; unless you change your mind," he winks. "You know I've always respected you."

"I'm being serious. No games." She turns on her heels. "I'm going to my room. Do not follow me."

"I hope you don't sleep for the entire weekend," he calls out. "We have Sicily to explore."

44

"Now unto him that is able to do exceeding abundantly above all that we ask or think, according to the power that worketh in us, unto him be glory in the church by Christ Jesus throughout all ages..." Ephesians 3:20-21

Vaia and Easton spent the rest of the day exploring Sicily. Jetlag didn't hit her as much as she'd expected. After lunch they had a mini photoshoot in the park.

"Smile babes," Easton encourages, while snapping a picture of Vaia. "Lovely. Are you enjoying yourself?"

"I know I didn't say it before, but thank you for this. I appreciate you helping me with a trip do over. You're really trying and it's not gone unnoticed."

"Anything for you. I love you, Vaia."

"Whoa," Vaia laughs. "Pull the brakes. We are not there yet. Let's not push it. One day at a time, okay?"

Easton stares into her eyes. "I never stopped loving you."

"We agreed to start over."

"From where we left off maybe, not from day one, year one," he counters.

Off in the distance a woman calls out Vaia's name.

"Do you know her?" Easton inquires, staring at the woman walking towards them.

Vaia turns to face the woman and gasps. "Arricia, what are you doing here?"

Arricia's eyes dart between Vaia and Easton. "I came to visit a friend. What are you doing back in Italy? Does my brother know that you're here?" She looks at Easton. "Is this your brother?"

"Brother? Oh no," Easton scoffs. "My name's Easton Tekir, Vaia's **fiancé**."

"Ex-fiancé," Vaia counters.

"Nice to meet you, Mr. Tekir." Arricia shakes his hand. "What are you two doing here?" she repeats.

"Pre-honeymoon scoping," Easton answers.

Vaia motions for his silence. "We're just enjoying a weekend getaway."

"You look good," Arricia compliments.

Easton places his hand around Vaia's waist. "Thanks to me."

Arricia smiles weakly. "I'll leave you two lovebirds alone. Nice seeing you again, Vaia."

165 Becoming a Royal Princess

"What were you trying to prove when you put your hand around me?"

"Who is she? What did she mean by *brother*?"

Vaia dusts off invisible crumbs from her face and whispers, "Princess Arricia of Lucca, Kalevi's sister."

"Why can't those royals leave you alone?" Easton states angrily.

"She didn't even know I was going to be here; unless you somehow made it public knowledge."

"You know that I'm a private man. Let's go." He grabs her hand.

"You don't have to pull me," Vaia retorts.

When Arricia enters the taxi, she immediately contacts her brother. *"Fratello, non crederesti a chi ho appena visto in Sicilia."*

"Who did you see?" Kalevi replies.

"Vaia and her **fiancé**."

45

"A fool uttereth all his mind: but a wise man keepeth it in till afterwards." Proverbs 29:11

Kalevi angrily hangs up his cell. **"She's engaged**?" he huffs.

"Who is?" Kavala inquires, walking into his study.

"Vaia."

Kavala rolls her eyes. "GET OVER IT!" she snaps. "She's clearly moved on and you're still pining over her. She doesn't want you. It took her all but **two** seconds to move on."

"I can't lose her. I want to work things out with her."

"You give that woman too much credit," Kavala responds, in disdain.

"I love her," he counters.

"Oh stop your whining. You're a grown man. Almost 33 and you're crying over a woman? Fix yourself up and let's talk about you and the baroness. You need to make an honest woman out of her. She's probably back home crying over you. Can't you see that she's the right woman for you to marry?"

"I don't love the baroness."

"You will marry her, Kalevi. This woman has loved you even before you married your first wife. You can't possibly be thinking about throwing away such a love for a foreign woman who's already moved on."

Kalevi stands up and proceeds to exit his study. "This conversation is daunting."

Kavala rushes in front of him. "No, allow me. You stay here. I'm going to call the baroness and see if she can return to the palace at once."

"If she comes back to this palace I'm leaving with my children," Kalevi states.

"Why don't you care about your mother's happiness? Why? What did I ever do?" Kavala whines.

"Get off the floor, mother. You're not an actress."

"Kinslee must return. I need a friend."

"No, you need Jesus." Kalevi walks past Kavala, leaving her to her antics.

46

"There hath no temptation taken you but such as is common to man: but God is faithful, who will not suffer you to be tempted above all that ye are able; but will with the temptation also make a way to escape, that ye may be able to bear it." 1 Corinthians 10:13

That night Easton and Vaia took a stroll through the Italian countryside.

"This has been a wonderful trip. I'm not ready to go back home," Vaia sighs.

Easton's phone rings. "Hold on a minute. I have to answer this." He turns to answer the call. "Yes sir. Uh huh. Yes. Sure. I'll send it over right away. Okay. I'll take the jet back after my trip. Bye."

Vaia stares up at him. "Where are you going?"

"Work crisis. I have to return home as soon as we land. I'll drop you to your house and then fly out."

"You chose work again?"

Easton takes her hand and gets down on his knee. "I should've done this the first time. Vaia, will you—"

"No," Vaia declines. "I will not marry you."

"I was going to say... will you come to my country with me? I know what you'd say about work and I've thought it through. You can teach anywhere. I can arrange a transfer for you. Give your boss two weeks so they can find a replacement."

"This isn't your decision. Besides, how could you expect me to leave my children?"

"They're not your children," he counters.

"Wow, thanks," Vaia's voice shakes.

"I didn't mean it that way."

"Yes you did. You know how sensitive I am about having children."

Easton hugs her. "You'll have children, Vaia. We'll pray and you'll have children. God is in charge."

Vaia steps back from his embrace. "Are you hearing yourself?"

"Did I say something wrong?" he mumbles.

"No. Y-you're actually being considerate. I never thought I'd see the day. You've changed."

Easton kisses her gently.

"Well alrighty then. Finally, progress." He stares up at the sky. "Let's go babe. I don't want you to get wet in the rain."

47

"For nothing is secret, that shall not be made manifest; neither any thing hid, that shall not be known and come abroad."
Luke 8:17

The following morning Vaia wakes up beside Easton on her bed. When she lifts the covers she notices they were both naked.

Oh no. What have we done?

She taps Easton on his shoulder. "Wake up. Wake up!"

Easton opens his eyes groggily. "H-huh? What is it?"

"Did we have sex last night?" she demands.

"I'm going back to sleep," he scoffs.

Vaia begins to cry. *Oh my gosh. I broke my promise to Jesus. I said I would not have sex again until I'm married. What if I get pregnant? I can't breathe. I can't breathe. Oh my gosh. Oh my gosh. I'm going to be sick...*

Jumping out of the bed, Vaia makes her way to the bathroom to throw up.

Lucca

"Madam, I think you'd want to see this."

"Not now Jarvis," Kavala declines.

"I've been doing an investigation," he continues.

"Why?"

He motions for Kavala to sit in the surveillance room. "I knew there was a reason I never liked Baroness Kinslee. It is my duty to protect this family and I have failed. I overheard her speaking on the phone planning her nuptials with the Crown Prince."

"What is wrong with that?" Kavala laughs. "I've been assisting her with those plans."

Jarvis types in the computer while talking to Kavala. "From the moment your son returned from his cruise trip I saw his countenance change. And when Ms. Bisenzo came in the palace I saw love in his eyes."

"Do not speak about that despicable woman," Kavala snaps.

"She's innocent, Your Highness," Jarvis blurts.

"What are you talking about?"

Jarvis points to the screen. "Come look at this."

Kavala stares at the screen. "What exactly am I looking at?"

"I've asked the security company to review the palace footage from the day Vaia arrived to her departure. They sent me a video that would dispel the accusation against her."

"Jarvis, I don't want to relive that horrible ordeal. That incident happened months ago. My granddaughter's safe now and out of that woman's evil clutches."

Ignoring her argument, he zooms in on the footage. "Pay attention to the date, time and **person** in this video."

"I don't have time for this," Kavala scoffs.

"It is your family's future at risk."

Kavala looks at the surveillance footage and gasps. "Is that the baroness? What is she doing?"

"Can't you see? She's tampering with the cake batter that was brought to your grandchildren. If you zoom in closer you can see two opened packets of *Thalak seeds* on the table."

"Impossible."

"Yes madam."

"The baroness?" she gulps.

Jarvis stands up to explain his investigation further. "As per protocol I search the bags of every guest that stays on the premises. When Ms. Bisenzo arrived at the palace, she did not have any seeds. *Thalak seeds* aren't something we have in Italy; it has to be ordered from Starr Islands. The baroness had enough time during her tenure to order the seeds and plot whatever unscrupulous scheme she had. Vaia only called one number, which turned out to be her mother. She did not use the internet or receive any packages while she stayed here, but Baroness Kinslee has on more than one occasion. I've asked my connection at the agency to search her deleted files and she did place an overnight order for two packets of the seeds the day before the incident. Also, the baroness would know of Kaveri's allergies, since she is a friend of the family."

"But why would she do something like this?

"Because madam, she wants to be the next Mrs. Kalevi Náousa."

"Kinslee isn't worthy of being married to my son. How DARE she attempt to kill my granddaughter! Doesn't she know that Kalevi's children are part of him? I must tell him this news at once. Get Detective Bruyére on the phone."

48

"And ye shall know the truth, and the truth shall make you free." John 8:32

Sunday Night

"How was your trip, honey?" Veria asks Vaia over the phone.

"I messed up," Vaia cries.

"What happened?"

"Easton and I had sex."

"This is—wonderful news," Veria gloats. "I hope he impregnated you."

"**Are you crazy**? I don't want to get pregnant before I'm married."

"Calm down, you're not a teenager. You're old enough to take care of a child."

"This can't be happening. I don't understand. I don't remember the drinks being that strong. I was careful."

Veria laughs. "My daughter, when hormones are raging and two people that are attracted to one another are in the same room, there's no telling what could happen."

"Why can't I remember anything?"

"Jetlag? I don't know. I wasn't there. But relax. Everything will be fine. Easton is a great man. You know he wants to marry you. Get married quickly so that your baby won't be a bastard."

"I'm not marrying him. Even if I become pregnant, I'll raise my baby alone."

"You're **not** going to be a single mother. Raising you and your brother was the hardest thing I ever did, but I did it. You don't have to make the same choice that I did. Why choose to be a single mother when you have a man who loves you and wants to marry you? That's folly."

"Key word here is *choice*," Vaia counters. "This is **my** choice. If I find out that I'm pregnant, I'm going to raise my child alone. I don't want to be in a loveless marriage just to save face."

"Loveless? Don't you love Easton?"

"No."

"When that bridge reaches we'll cross it," Veria scoffs. "Where is he now?"

"Take a guess."

"Back home?"

"He's already made his decision. He was so silent on the flight back as if I disgusted him."

"Maybe he was tired," Veria replies.

"Sex is a big deal to me. I don't want to just—"

"You already did it many times with Easton before you broke up. It's not a big deal."

"It is to me now. I have a lot of repentance to do. This cannot happen again."

"Well, you should've thought of that before you went on a trip with him. Things can happen."

"MOM!"

"Good night Vaia. I'll talk to you tomorrow. This is exciting news." Veria clicks off the phone.

49

"But if ye forgive not men their trespasses, neither will your Father forgive your trespasses." Matthew 6:15

Back at the palace, Kavala stopped her son at the front door. "Kalevi, can we speak?"

"I'm headed to the jailhouse."

"Go get her!" Kavala exclaims.

"Who?"

"Vaia."

Kalevi stares at his mother. "She's engaged to another man. I have enough on my plate."

"Listen son," Kavala laments. "I've made a lot of mistakes in my life. And shunning Vaia was one of them. She's been so kind to me, even though sassy at times. But, she's never disrespected me. She loves your children, I can see it. A mother knows. Vaia loves you. I'm sorry that I brought Kinslee into the palace. I will never forgive myself for the part I played in her actions. Have me arrested too. I don't deserve to live among you. I couldn't even protect my own family from a master manipulator."

"Kinslee's actions aren't your fault. I know you wouldn't deliberately hurt your family."

"I gave her something for you to drink from the apothecary so that you can fall in love with her," Kavala admits.

"I forgive you."

"Did you hear what I said? I gave her something."

"I heard you. The most important thing is for you to ask God for forgiveness. HE's the one whose help you need."

"I will do that. But. Go. Get. Her. You may not get this opportunity again."

"I'm going to the jailhouse," Kalevi refuses. "We'll talk about Vaia no further."

"Papa, can I ask you a question?"

Kalevi stops from turning the doorknob. "What is it Milos?"

"Is something wrong with *signorina*?"

Kalevi tries to come up with a quick response. "Why do you ask?"

"I don't see her anymore. And we don't call her on the phone like before," he says, tears welling up in his eyes. "Is she alive? Did she go to heaven like *mamma*?"

Kneeling down, Kalevi puts his hand on Milos' shoulder. "*Signorina* is fine, but we aren't speaking to one another."

"But why?" Milos asks.

"Well, you see—"

"Does this have to do with Baroness Kinslee? Do you like her instead of *signorina*? Is she going to be our new *mamma*?"

Kalevi's eyes widen. "Why do you think that?"

"I may be young, but I see things," Milos answers. "I don't really understand it, but I need a new *mamma*, so do something. Ok?" Milos says, tapping his father's shoulder.

What am I going to do? I can't explain to him the real reason that Vaia and I won't work. Oh well, I can't think about that now. I have to go to the jailhouse...

Legno di Corvo Jailhouse

"Kalevi, you came to see me," Kinslee squeals. "Are you going to free me from these shackles? I don't like it in here." She wrinkles her nose. "It smells like poverty. I'm ready for us to get married."

"I never knew you to behave this way."

"You didn't come here to free me?"

"I came to say that I forgive you," Kalevi replies.

"F-forgive me?" Kinslee stammers.

Kalevi looks at her with sadness in his eyes. "Holding on to the pain you caused wouldn't change anything. My daughter is alive and well, but there are consequences for your actions and we must adhere to the law."

Kinslee begins to cry. "I wanted to be a Crown Princess. Was it wrong of me, to want a new status in life? I do love you, Kalevi. Even before your wife. You met us both, yet you chose her. Why?"

"Love cannot be explained."

"I always resented her for taking away my chances of becoming a princess."

"I pray that you let go of the hatred you have towards Sivōrï." He pauses to reflect before continuing, "She's no longer with us, but you shouldn't live your life with bitterness in your heart."

"All I wanted was for us to be together," Kinslee mumbles. "I didn't want your children. They remind me of her. I wanted them to go to boarding school so that we could start over with children of our own."

"My children are part of me. And I would never send them away. If you truly loved me, you'd have loved my children as well. You don't know what love is. My prayer is that you give your life to Jesus and ask God to heal you from your bitterness."

"GET OUT OF HERE," Kinslee shouts. "I'VE ENDURED ENOUGH HUMILIATION AT THE HANDS OF YOUR FAMILY."

"Good bye Kinslee," Kalevi states. "I really hope that you get the help you need and I'll be praying for you."

50

"Ask, and it shall be given you; seek, and ye shall find; knock, and it shall be opened unto you..." Matthew 7:7

Friday

Kalevi and Arricia boarded their private jet.

"Thanks for accompanying me," Kalevi states.

"I'm happy to share this moment with you. Vaia is a wonderful woman and would make a great addition to our family. Took you long enough to fight for her," Arricia responds.

"I know," Kalevi nods. "I wonder what she'll say when she sees me?"

"Your dinner, sir," the chef on board announces.

"Thank you." Kalevi takes the tray from the chef and looks over at his sister. "What are you reading?"

Arricia closes down her laptop. "I don't think you want to see this."

"What is it?"

"Don't look," she replies. "It's not good."

Kalevi takes the laptop and opens it. "Let me see."

"Okay, if you insist," Arricia whispers.

VOQUE REAL ESTATE TYCOON, EASTON TEKIR MARRIES HIS LONG TIME SWEEATHEART, LUX POINT MILANO TEACHER, VAIA BISENZO

"She got married?" Kalevi whimpers.

"I'm sorry brother," Arricia says. "I guess we're too late."

"Did Vaia share anything with you about this Easton person?"

Arricia shakes her head.

"Then I shall have Jarvis do some research."

"Wait a minute..."

"What is it?" Kalevi asks.

"Let me check online." She types in Easton's name in the search engine. "According to *FindIt.help*, Easton was born in *Voque*. He is the son of a major real estate developer based in Lithuania. He grew up there and moved back to Starr Islands when he was offered a lucrative position in a top firm five years ago. Vaia surely knows how to pick them," Arricia chuckles.

"What is that supposed to mean?"

"Girl code," Arricia shrugs. "So what are you going to do about this news?"

"Absolutely nothing." Kalevi motions for the air hostess. "Tell the pilot to turn this plane around at once."

Arricia's eyes widen. "Wait, what?"

"I'm not going to fight for a married woman. We'll speak of this to no one," he states, peering out the window.

The plane had only been in the air for two hours when Kalevi asked the pilot to ground it.

When he arrived back at the palace, Kavala stares in bewilderment. "My son, you're back rather quickly. Did Vaia come here instead? Where is she?"

"Probably on her honeymoon," Kalevi grumbles.

"What are you talking about?"

"It's over," Kalevi admits to his mother. "I took too long. She's married now. Mrs. Vaia Tekir."

"Tekir?"

"That's her husband's last name."

"I'm so sorry. This is my fault," Kavala sighs.

"Stop blaming yourself for her choice. She made her decision."

"If I didn't reject her, she would've been here with you."

"It doesn't matter anymore. Everything turned out the way it was supposed to."

"I'm going to fix this," his mother announces.

"Forget it. Let her live in peace."

Seeing her son as an emotional wreck was one thing, knowing it was her fault made Kavala cringe on the inside.

As a mother it was her duty to protect her children. Although she knew Kalevi would disapprove, she wanted to hear from Vaia about her alleged nuptials. Immediately after he left the room, Kavala dials Vaia's number.

"Hello?" Vaia answers. "Who is this?"

"Good evening, may I please speak with Vaia Bisenzo?"

"Dowager Princess Kavala?"

"I guess congratulations are in order," Kavala retorts.

"Congratulations for what?"

"Aren't you officially Mrs. Tekir? I'm surprised that you picked up your phone. I thought you'd be on your honeymoon by now," Kavala blurts.

"What are you talking about?" Vaia asks. "When did I get married?"

"It's all over the internet. Vaia Bisenzo is now Mrs. Easton Tekir."

185 Becoming a Royal Princess

"I'm not married," Vaia scoffs. "Easton's not even in the country. I'm confused. Hold on, let me check." Vaia types in a search of their names. "What on earth?"

"So you're not married?" Kavala reiterates.

"No, I'm not."

Kavala smiles. "This is great news."

"I thought you hated me?"

"We have a lot to discuss..."

"Hello? Hello?"

Did she just hang up on me? Wait, what's going on?

51

"And he that taketh not his cross, and followeth after me, is not worthy of me. He that findeth his life shall lose it: and he that loseth his life for my sake shall find it." Matthew 10:38-39

The conversation with Kavala made Vaia seething mad. She walked around her kitchen wondering why Easton would put up false information about their relationship.

The doorbell rang just as she picked up her phone to give him a piece of her mind. Putting down the device, Vaia walks to the door.

She opens it and greets her guest with a repulsed face. "I'm not in the mood."

"That's not the greeting I expected," Easton replies, kissing her cheek.

"I shouldn't allow you inside, but we need to talk."

"I have something to ask you."

"You can go first."

"Vaia, I love you so much. All that I've done for these past few weeks is to show you how much I want us to work. You're beautiful, smart, loyal, and truly fun to be around. You make me laugh and you get me. I don't want to be with any other. The reason I went home is to finalize my job transfer here. I know you love living in *Lux Point Milano* and I want you to be happy, teaching your children. Marry me Vaia, tomorrow. Everything's already arranged," Easton proposes.

"Are you out of your mind?" Vaia snaps. "I don't want to marry you. I see however, that you've already shared the *news* with the world. There's an article online saying that we got married."

"Oh no," Easton smacks his forehead, "you saw my surprise. That was for tomorrow. They got the date wrong."

"You deliberately put up my information without my knowledge? You know that I value my privacy."

"We're on the same page when it comes to privacy, but one's marriage isn't something to hide. I want the world to know how much I love you."

"I'm sorry that you think there's something between us, but I really don't feel a connection with you. My heart belongs to someone else," she sighs. "And now I have to go to the doctor for a pregnancy test."

"Pregnancy test? Are you pregnant, **for him**?"

"No you goofball." Vaia rolls her eyes. "You're the father."

"That's impossible."

"Didn't we have sex on our final night in Sicily?"

"No we didn't," Easton huffs.

"Easton, I'm asking a serious question. Stop playing around."

"As much as I would've loved to have a pre-honeymoon rendezvous with the woman I love, it didn't happen. I couldn't have sex with a woman who called another man's name aloud. You were a little tipsy and started kissing me. I was enjoying the moment, but then you called out **Kalevi's** name. That was an instant turn off for me. Then we went to your room and you vomited all over my clothes, crying that you should not have had any alcohol and you passed out on the bed."

Vaia stares at him in disbelief. She wasn't pregnant. But, a question still plagued her mind. "How'd I end up naked?"

"I did try to do something before you vomited. We got as far as second base and then you called his name again; over and over. I'd had enough. I was too tired to go down to my room, so I just slept on your bed."

"This is a relief," Vaia exclaims. "We didn't have sex. WE DID NOT HAVE SEX. OH MY GOSH. I'M NOT PREGNANT. THANK YOU JESUS!" She jumps up in excitement.

"Would you keep it down?" Easton asks. "This is an utter embarrassment to my manhood."

"You don't understand. This is great news."

Easton holds up the ring once more. "Is your final answer **no**?"

"Yes."

"Your final answer is **yes**?"

189 Becoming a Royal Princess

Vaia shakes her head. "You love your work. I won't be second to your career. I hope that one day you find what you are looking for. For starters, you need a relationship with Jesus. Not just going to church. We've wasted enough of each other's time. It's time I get my life back on track. Good bye Easton."

Easton puts the ring back in his pocket and kisses her hand. "Good bye Vaia. I hope you get the love that you deserve."

Vaia closes the door to her ex for the second time in less than two years.

First things first: a time of prayer and fasting. I need to spend some time with Jesus. Enough men drama...

52

"Then came Peter to him, and said, Lord, how oft shall my brother sin against me, and I forgive him? till seven times? Jesus saith unto him, I say not unto thee, until seven times: but, until seventy times seven." Matthew 18:21-22

December 2nd

Veria joined her daughter for lunch. "How are you feeling honey?"

"Mom, I've never felt better. I feel free of all my thirtieth year drama. My birthday is next month and I'm good. I have decided to go to Australia for my next trip."

"Good for you baby. You're smiling more."

"The fast was worth it," Vaia smiles.

"I noticed that you've been studying that Bible of yours, a lot. Do you want to share some of what you learned?" Veria asks.

"Sure." Vaia smiled at the opportunity to speak about the Bible with her mother. "I felt led to study the Book of Esther."

"Who's Esther and why is she important? I didn't know the Bible had books about women."

"The Bible talks about everything under the sun. You name it, there's a verse or chapter for it. And the Bible has two books that highlight women specifically; **Esther** and **Ruth**. Of course there are other women whose stories are mentioned throughout the Bible."

"Tell me more about this Esther," Veria inquires.

"Esther was known as Hadassah at birth, but her name was changed before she became the Queen of Persia to hide her Jewish identity."

"A queen huh. Just like my baby girl."

Vaia giggles. "Thanks mom."

"Well… continue. I want to hear more about this queen."

"What was significant about Esther's story was that she was an orphan, raised by her older cousin Mordecai. He is the one who encouraged her to become a queen. You see, the king had a wife named Vashti who disrespected him in front of his friends. After this humiliation, they advised him to divorce her to make a public demonstration, so that their wives wouldn't try usurping their authority—"

"Ohhhh, the Bible has drama **drama**," Veria notes.

"I told you mom, the Bible has everything. After Vashti was **disposed** of, so to speak, a competition was held in the land for all virgins to vie for the position of being the king's second wife. In the end, although the odds were against Esther, she won the competition and became the Queen of Persia; which by the way had over one hundred provinces."

"That's amazing. It sounds a little like your situation with the prince. A chance at being his second wife, except I'm sure his first wife wasn't like this Vashti woman. And you also come from a different background. Now that's a very interesting choice for a Bible study."

"I felt led to study that book for my entire time of fasting."

"I see. Well you look good. Not so depressed as when you returned from Italy after that whole debacle with the prince's daughter."

Trying to change the topic, for fear of her thoughts wandering to Kalevi, Vaia asks her mom, "Will you be joining me for tonight's church service?"

"Sure," Veria shrugs.

"Really?" Vaia gasps.

Veria nods. "I figured that I have nothing to lose. You've gone through so much and still want to serve this Jesus. HE must be some man."

"HE's the **best**," Vaia blushes. "I love HIM."

"Well, what are we waiting for? What time does it start?"

"7PM."

"I'll be there," her mother replies.

"I'm happy to hear you say that," Vaia squeals.

After her mother leaves, Vaia puts her phone to charge while she sat to read a book.

Suddenly, the doorbell rings.

I seem to have a lot of visitors these days.

Placing her book on the table, Vaia proceeds to open the front door.

"Good day Vaia," Kavala greets.

Vaia's eyes widen. "Dowager Princess Kavala? What are you doing here?"

"May I come in?"

"Are you here by yourself?" Vaia asks, looking around for Kalevi.

"Of course not; Jarvis is outside waiting in the limo."

Vaia tries to hide her disappointment. "Would you like some *Cobalt Tea*?"

"I hope there are no *Thalak seeds* in it."

Vaia grimaces. "Let's not talk about that."

"My apologies," Kavala replies. "Lovely place you've got here. You have excellent taste."

"*Grazie*," Vaia replies in Italian. "To what do I owe the pleasure of your visit?"

"Come back to Italy," Kavala requests.

"I don't think I'm welcomed there. Too much has taken place. I'm going to stay in Starr Islands," Vaia declines.

"Love is a risk."

"Love?"

"I'm speaking about my son. Normally, I wouldn't do this. But, I must apologize for my atrocious non-lady like behavior. It was unbecoming of me as a woman, Dowager Crown Princess, mother, and grandmother. How I treated you was inappropriate. Kalevi loves you. And I would never forgive myself if I didn't try to assist in a small way to get you two back together. Ultimately it's your decision— what I'm trying to say is... Vaia, can you forgive me? I would be honored if you would join our family. I couldn't ask for a better daughter-in-law," Kavala beseeches.

"I thought you hated me?"

"I didn't allow myself to get to know you. As a monarch, I come in contact with people from all over the world, but I never got to know anyone who didn't look like me. That was a mistake I made. When my husband was alive he made a lot of changes that I disagreed with. Although I didn't want to admit it, he was at peace. He opened his heart to people of all backgrounds. When I saw you, it reminded me of him and how betrayed I felt. I know it was stupid, but I've done a lot of soul searching and I'm learning to open my heart to people, starting with you. Please come back..."

Vaia begins to cry. "I would love nothing better than to do that, but what purpose will I have to be there? I haven't spoken to Kalevi in months. I don't even think he'll want me anymore. Not after all that has happened."

"Worry not about the future. I'm planning a party for him. As you know his birthday is January 1st. I'll arrange for you to fly in on New Year's Eve and as the clock strikes midnight, you'll descend the stairs into the ballroom. I can just picture it now. I want you to be his surprise. I'd be sure to get *Mother of The Year.*"

"You're serious?"

"When it comes to my family, I do not joke," Kavala replies.

"I will pray about it," Vaia states.

"Do what you must."

"Thank you Dowager Princess Kavala."

"Am I forgiven?"

"Yes," Vaia replies, hugging Kavala.

Is this really happening? Did I just get her approval?

53

"And above all things have fervent charity among yourselves: for charity shall cover the multitude of sins." 1 Peter 4:8

December 31ˢᵗ

"You look good brother," Arricia compliments. "We're almost in 2023. Excited?"

"I'm thankful," Kalevi answers. "I've been through a lot this year. But, I made it with God's help. I'm blessed with beautiful children, my mother, and you my sister. What more could a man ask for?"

"Papa, do you like my dress?"

Kalevi smiles at his daughter. "Kaveri, you're a true princess. You look beautiful."

"Thank you papa," Kaveri blushes.

"Where's your brother?"

"In the kitchen, eating cake," she giggles.

"Is he eating from my birthday cake?"

"No, the chef baked him a special cake for being his helper in making your cake," Kaveri laughs.

"Go get your brother. The countdown is starting soon," Kalevi informs his daughter.

"It's almost midnight," Kavala announces.

"2023, here we come. Thanks mother. I know we have our differences, but I love you. Thanks for all that you do for me and the children."

"You are my favorite son."

"I'm your only son," Kalevi replies.

"You don't know that."

"Mother?"

"I'm joking. Everyone said that I am **stiff**," she laughs. "I'm trying something new, sarcasm."

"Don't joke about those things. Time to countdown," Kalevi turns on the mic.

"10...9...8...7..." Kalevi and his guests begin.

As the clock struck midnight, the crowd gasps.

Kalevi wondered what made everyone so astonished. He turns his attention to the stairway behind him. The mic dropped from his hand. There she was, dressed like a queen; the one who had his heart. "Vaia," was all he said as the tears began to fall.

All eyes were on her as she announced, "Happy Birthday and New Year, Kalevi."

"Vaia?" he repeats, running to her. "Is this real? Am I dreaming?"

"No," Vaia replies through tears. "This is not a dream. I'm really here."

For a moment, time stood still as he took in her beauty.

"Are you surprised?" she asks softly.

He hugs her. "I sure am."

Vaia continues to cry as they stare at one another.

Kalevi falls on his knees, asking her forgiveness for his irrational behavior and utter stupidity. "Vaia, I am so sorry for all the hurt that I've caused you; for being inconsiderate of your feelings and what you were going through. I'm sorry for being a hypocrite in not trusting you when you were trying to tell me that you had nothing to do with Kaveri's hospitalization. Forgive me for thinking so low of you. Knowing the woman you are; you'd never do something like that. I was a fool for ever asking you to leave, for letting you go. Can you please forgive me?"

"I forgive you, Kalevi," Vaia utters as tears continued to stream down her face.

Kalevi stands up and straightens his tie. "I have one question. And please know that I'm happy, but I just need to know... Who invited you?"

Vaia turns to Kavala. "Your mother invited me."

Kalevi's eyes widen.

Kavala motions for him to continue conversing with Vaia. "This isn't about me. The love of your life is standing right in front of you. Kiss her already."

Kalevi takes Vaia in his arms and they share a passionate kiss.

Taking her face in his hands, he pours out his heart to Vaia. "*Ti amo moltissimo. Tu sei la mia regina,*" he says in Italian.

Vaia giggles. "And you are my king."

"This is the **best** present ever. May I say you look even more stunning? Turn around, turn around, and let me have a look. *Sei bellissima amore mio.* Beautiful," Kalevi compliments.

"Oh behave," Vaia blushes.

He laughs.

Arricia hugs Vaia. "I'm happy that you are here."

Kalevi looks at his sister. "You knew about this?"

"Who do you think gave mother Vaia's phone number?"

"Who else knew?"

"**Everyone**," Arricia replies.

"The children?"

"Yes," she nods.

"Aren't they too young to keep such a huge secret?"

"That's why we told them this morning. We didn't want to put too much pressure on them," Arricia chuckles.

Vaia smiles and looks at Kalevi. "God answered my prayer."

"Me?"

"Sort of. I asked HIM if it's HIS will for me to start off 2023 with the one HE has for me."

"*Mio amore*, that's a beautiful prayer."

Vaia blushes.

Kalevi extends his hand. "Shall we dance?"

"Yes," Vaia nods. "It's time for me to dance with my love in Lucca..."

As Vaia twirled around the dance floor, she reflected on all the years of disappointments she'd endured in relationships. She never thought that she'd be a part of something bigger than herself. Yet here she was dancing with God's son, The Crown Prince of Lucca; a man of noble birth.

She now understood the definition of what it meant to be royalty. It wasn't about an earthly title. Many women wouldn't get the opportunity to marry an earthly royal. But she realized something while she danced with Kalevi in front of all the Italian dignitaries: the moment that she accepted Jesus Christ as her Lord and Savior, is when she truly became a **Royal Princess**.

And that was a lesson she'd never forget. She was royalty **before** she met her husband.

"For this cause shall a man leave father and mother, and shall cleave to his wife..." Matthew 19:5

HRH Dowager Crown Princess Kavala of Lucca
invite

_____

_____

to the Marriage of
His Royal Highness Crown Prince Kalevi of Lucca
with
Miss Vaia Bisenzo
at Chiesa del Regno
on Monday, May 1st, 2023 at 10 a.m.

A reply is requested to:
Segretario del Palazzo - Palazzo di Náousa
Dress: Formal

203 Becoming a Royal Princess

A Note from the Author

The world we live in equates self-worth/value to material things, accomplishments, wealth, status, etc. But deep down in our hearts we know that those things do not fill the emptiness we experience at times. So many people have acquired status, fame, wealth, titles behind their names and yet, they still feel empty.

Although this is a fictional story and Vaia's journey was sweet and at times cringe worthy, I can identify with her journey; having experienced rejection from my ex-boyfriends, bad dates, inappropriate conversations with men, and a border wars type of heartbreak. Having previously battled with low self-esteem as a result of these experiences, I know all too well how certain situations can change your viewpoint of expecting something more (the best from God).

At the age of 16 I was given the nickname *Empress* by an older woman who saw value in me when I felt like an ugly duckling. It took many years for me to truly internalize what the name meant. It wasn't **just** a nickname. The name signified who I am in Christ. I just didn't know it at that time.

Over a decade has passed since I embraced my identity and I can say that I truly am an Empress; understanding that the King of Kings is my Father. Christ is the **only** One who can define me.

I learned that the voids in my life cannot be filled through earthly relationships. Only a relationship with Christ can fill those voids.

I am **Royalty**, chosen by God to be HIS Ambassador on the earth. I've learned that I was created by God for a purpose and that everything that I have gone through was not in vain. This is what matters. Being **chosen** and selected by God for Kingdom business.

No matter what stage you are in your life, always remember that you were created for **more**. If you want to know who you *truly* are, ask God. Pray, read HIS word, and spend time with HIM.

When you know who you are and who you belong to, no one can call you out of your name.

I know who I am. Royalty. An Empress. God's Ambassador. Daughter of the Most High God, Theastarr.

There's no need to wait for *"Prince Charming"* to define me, when my identity is found in the Creator of the Universe... The King of Kings Himself, Jesus Christ.

I'd like to remind every reader that you are special to the Creator of the Universe and HE loves you. In Christ you are indeed **Royalty**.

~Theastarr Valerie

Bonus

Using the next few pages, write a note to your younger (or current self) sharing some of the lessons you've learned along life's journey. What did you experience? How did it shape your outlook on life? What have you learned about your identity? What defines you? Then at the end, write down a Bible verse (or verses) that you can look back at when you're battling with doubts of inadequacy.

Journal Entry

Dear

_____

_____

_____

_____

_____

_____

_____

_____

_____

_____

_____

_____

_____

_____

_____

Love,

Other books by Theastarr

The Road That Led To Love

What's worse than loving a man who doesn't know you exist?

*Tahira Zagori had everything life had to offer; loving parents, a wonderful best friend, career and her own home. There was only one thing missing, according to her **mother**... A HUSBAND!!*

What happens when you give into the pressures of others? What happens when you choose not to listen to God?

When God writes your love story, it's more beautiful than you could ever imagine.

The road that leads to love is never easy, but always...
WORTH THE WAIT!!

Story Sample

I never met him, but I'm completely in love with him. When I was 8 years old I saw him for the first time on TV. I watched every show and movie he acted in and swooned. He is THE definition of FINATION. I had to make up a word to describe him. Yes, I know wishful thinking. As if I would EVER meet him. As if he would EVER like me...

"Earth to Tahira," Kaiora sings.

"We are supposed to be studying," Tahira replies. Kaiora Marzocco had been Tahira's firecracker best friend for the past two years. Her mouth was known to get her in trouble at times; she held nothing back.

"I know that, but you zoned out. Daydreaming about that boy again?" she jeers.

"Who?" Tahira asks.

"The one you've liked since you were 8 years old."

"No. I was pondering on our exam tomorrow."

"Good. You need to learn now that it will never happen. Our life isn't a movie. Boys like that don't court or marry regular girls like us," Kaiora scolded, while popping a gum in her mouth.

Tahira stands up and declares, "I am not a regular girl. I am the daughter of a King."

"So am I, but the Bible speaks about idolatry."

"I haven't idolized anyone."

"Either way, let's stick with reality," Kaiora states nonchalantly.

"Besides, he isn't a believer."

Tahira frowns. "He does believe in Jesus."

"Believing in Jesus and serving HIM are two different things."

"Can we stop with the sermons? I know God's word," Tahira conveys, becoming agitated.

Pointing to the textbooks Kaiora ends the conversation. "Back to our studies."

Tahira begins to twiddle her fingers, zoning Kaiora out as she thinks.

Why is it so impossible for me to marry Tavario Mikos? He could become a Christian, like really serving Jesus. SIGH!! Who am I kidding? As Kaiora said, this isn't the movies...

End of Sample.

Murder In Zaire Valley

A secret kept for 40 years.

A wife imprisoned for killing her husband.

An amateur sleuth.

Carvings. Hidden agendas. Threats. Animosity.
MURDER!!

PhD graduate Nhyira Enosis is no stranger to murder. Inside the walls of her newly purchased home lies the truth about a 40-year-old homicide.

Can she convince the police to open up a case that has long stigmatized the citizens of Zaire Valley? Or will she be the latest victim of a flawed justice system...

Story Sample

Flipping through the radio stations, Nhyira Enosis puts her **Epitome X Series 1** into sports mode, excited at the chance to test drive her new car. She was minutes away from her potential dream house: a 40-year-old mansion in *Njapa, Zaire Valley,* Celgagoas.

A native of *Grape Fjord,* Mt. Thafivin, she was known as **The** Spelling Bee Champ. Nhyira had a natural ability to unscramble any word from the dictionary.

And no one could deny her fascination for unsolved mysteries. When she read the ad for the abandoned house up for auction, she knew that it had to be hers.

With her inheritance in her purse she mashed the gas pedal. If she missed the auction, someone else would bid on the house. That was a setback she couldn't afford.

Mr. Sellers had the perfect house for Nhyira. As the top Real Estate Agent in *Zaire Valley*, he knew how to match the perfect house with its perfect owner. This particular house however, remained unsold for decades. No one in the country was interested in procuring a house formerly owned by a man whose wife murdered him in cold blood.

The mystery of the old **Veisiejai House** remained since 1958. It was a part of *Njapa's* history that none of its residents dared to speak about. Only a handful of citizens knew what *really* happened on that fateful night...

End of Sample.

Follow **Empress Royále Publishing** on Facebook and Instagram for information about upcoming books from Theastarr Valerie.

www.ingramcontent.com/pod-product-compliance
Lightning Source LLC
Chambersburg PA
CBHW032000240626
47153CB00003B/1051